FIRST-Y

Nurse Phyllida Sims, helplessly accident-prone since
she began work on the wards at Hartlake Hospital, is
known to her friends as a walking disaster area. So
when she falls in love with Ross Harman, a rakish
registrar of high ambition, the outcome seems inevitable.

Books you will enjoy
in our Doctor–Nurse series

FIRST-YEAR'S FANCY

BY

LYNNE COLLINS

MILLS & BOON LIMITED
London · Sydney · Toronto

First published in Great Britain 1983
by Mills & Boon Limited, 15–16 Brook's Mews,
London W1A 1DR

© Lynne Collins 1983

Australian copyright 1983
Philippine copyright 1983

ISBN 0 263 74254 7

Set in 10 on 12 pt Linotron Times
03/0483

Photoset by Rowland Phototypesetting Ltd
Bury St Edmunds, Suffolk
Made and printed in Great Britain by
Richard Clay (The Chaucer Press) Ltd
Bungay, Suffolk

CHAPTER ONE

PHYLLIDA was late.

Even worse, the cap with its one blue stripe of the first-year nurse was slowly sliding over one ear as it did too often. That cap was the bane of her life.

And, worst of all, Ross Harman was on the ward. He was talking to the senior staff nurse when Phyllida hurtled through the swing doors with her usual breathless haste, flushed and flustered because she had spent too long talking to Jimmy, the Head Porter who knew everything about everybody at Hartlake and was probably the main root of the hospital grapevine.

Ross Harman raised a coolly amused eyebrow and she felt about thirteen. She clutched at her wayward cap, face flaming with guilt although he could not possibly know that he had been the subject of her conversation with Jimmy.

'You're late, Nurse Sims.' Georgy Knight was not very pleased that a quiet moment with the attractive registrar had been so rudely interrupted. There were not many moments for a little harmless flirtation on a busy ward.

'Yes, Staff. I'm sorry, Staff.' The response was automatic. Phyllida was carefully not meeting a pair of dark eyes with an engaging twinkle in their depths.

Her cap slipped another inch. It was all the fault of the shining chestnut hair, smooth as silk and as slippery as an ice rink for a ridiculous trifle of starched linen. Her hands were clasped behind her back in the traditionally demure pose of the well-trained nurse. Phyllida hastily crossed her fingers and sent up a silent prayer for good measure. But the wilful cap slithered and fell to the floor for all her efforts.

Ross Harman chuckled.

Georgy's grey eyes snapped irritation. Phyllida hastily stooped to retrieve the cap and the hairpins that had quite failed to keep it in place. 'Sorry, Staff . . .'

She thought wryly that she spent much of her time on the ward apologising for one thing or another. She loved nursing, but somehow she had become hopelessly accident-prone since she began work on the wards.

She had enjoyed the weeks in Preliminary Training School, passing the first examinations with flying colours and looking forward eagerly to the wards and the real work of nursing. She was a quick learner with a retentive memory, interested and enthusiastic and keen to do well. But theory and practice had turned out to be very different things.

Her fellow juniors called her a walking disaster area, gently teasing. For if there was a thermometer to be dropped and broken, or a feeding-cup to be spilled or knocked out of a patient's hand, or a trolley to be upset when it was laid in readiness for a dressing or an injection or suture removal, or someone to be barged into when emerging from kitchen or sluice or linen cupboard, then Phyllida was your girl! She was the despair of her seniors and a comedy turn to her friends.

But she promised to be an excellent nurse in other ways. She was kind and gentle and caring and she seemed to have an instant rapport with the patients. Everyone liked her bright smile and willing ways. Nothing was ever too much trouble for Phyllida.

It was that impulsive eagerness to please and to be of real use that was her downfall. Wanting to do the work of a dozen nurses, she seldom had enough time to complete her own because she was constantly clearing up after silly and irritating accidents. None so very serious that she was a danger to the patients, but any one of them enough to make a sister or staff nurse exclaim with justified exasperation that she would never make a nurse.

Now, Georgy Knight looked her up and down with cold disapproval stamped all over a rather lovely face. Phyllida felt like a naughty schoolgirl.

'You should know better than to come on duty in that dishevelled condition, Nurse. Go off the ward and make yourself tidy and then report to me again!'

'Yes, Staff. I'm sorry, Staff.' Phyllida stifled a sigh, wondering why she seemed to alienate the staff nurse without even trying. For some reason, Georgy just didn't like her and wasn't prepared to make allowances. Fortunately, Sister did or she would be on Matron's Report almost every day!

As she turned away, her elbow just brushed the pile of folders that were balanced precariously on the edge of the desk. She made a hasty grab for the top folder as it threatened to topple. Ross Harman was a fraction faster. As their hands briefly touched, he smiled at her with a little sympathy.

Georgy uttered a small, sharply impatient sound that might or might not have been prompted by the near-disaster. Phyllida did not dare to smile back at the registrar while the staff nurse was looking such daggers.

He returned the folder to the pile and thoughtfully straightened the rest. He had strong, very muscular yet sensitive-shaped hands . . . the hallmark of a surgeon. He was reputed to be a very good surgeon, aiming for a consultancy.

Phyllida found herself making another rueful apology before she hurried from the ward. She knew that they had their heads together before the swing doors closed behind her. Sister was off duty. As the senior staff nurse, Georgy was responsible for the running of the ward in her absence. It might be supposed that doctor and nurse were earnestly discussing the patients. Phyllida knew better. She had seen that particular sparkle in the staff nurse's eyes whenever Professor Wilson's registrar came into the ward.

Ross Harman was so good-looking that it was almost a pity that he seemed to have no time at all for first-years like herself, Phyllida mused, struggling with her cap in the juniors' room. He reserved his amorous attentions for senior staff and it was rumoured that he was very amorous and very attentive—while it lasted! He was dangerously attractive and much too light-hearted and fickle for any girl's peace of mind, apparently. Or, like many ambitious young doctors, too wary of serious involvement to stay faithful to one girl for long.

Hartlake was famous for the prettiness as well as the skill and efficiency of its nurses. There were plenty of attractive girls to catch the roving eye of a Casanova. Doctors tended to marry nurses not only because they were thrown in each other's way but also because a nurse was conscious of the demands and difficulties of a doctor's life and knew what to expect.

Doctors like Ross Harman who had no thought of marriage tended to pursue nurses for the same reasons. Long hours of duty and intense concentration on ward or in theatre or clinic meant that a man needed to relax and unwind at the end of the day. Preferably with a pretty girl who knew and understood the pressures of the job and made allowances for the unexpected emergency that could distrupt plans at the last minute.

Phyllida looked into the deep blue eyes that looked ruefully back at her as she stood before the mirror in the juniors' room. There was no future in fancying Ross Harman, she told herself firmly. She was too young and too inexperienced to appeal to his kind. It would be silly to attach the least importance to the charm in a smile that he bestowed on anything in a skirt!

But he was rather nice, Phyllida thought wistfully. Dangerous but nice. She could not help quickening with a little excitement whenever she met the smile in his eyes. Like too many girls, of course. She had no illusions about him. He looked like a rake with those glinting dark eyes and that sensual mouth and the swift spark of interest in that handsome face whenever he looked at an attractive woman. He *was* a rake, according to the hospital grapevine. It might exaggerate, but there was always a grain of truth in the rumours.

She sighed and tugged at her apron and knew she ought not to be dawdling when there was so much work to be done and never enough hands. Paterson was a busy ward with its steady flow of admissions, the almost daily preparation of patients for Theatres, the need for half-

hourly observations on post-operative patients, the con-
tinual call for nurses to special the very ill—and, of
course, the never-ending rounds. Drugs, pulse and
temps, b.p.'s, dressings, bedpans and washings, fluid
charts, bedmaking and back rubs and blanket baths,
meals and hot drinks. At times, it seemed an endless list
of chores to get through, but a nurse had to smile and
carry on even when feet, back and sometimes heart
ached almost beyond bearing.

Then there were doctors' rounds and teaching rounds.
The latter could be very disruptive to routine for patients
were unsettled and nurses distracted by a group of
students wandering about the ward.

Sister Hamilton was good-natured and cheerful and
easy-going for all her brisk and practical and very
efficient running of the ward. Her predecessor, Ruth
Challis, had married a consultant, inspiring hope in the
hearts of some of the young nurses who were more
interested in men than in medicine and easily impressed
by the glamour of a white coat. Most of the consultants
were elderly or married or both, however, and not very
likely to give a second glance to a junior nurse. So all
their flirtatious efforts were centred on men like Ivor
Maynard and Todd Morgan and Ross Harman, attractive and eligible bachelors who made the most of their
many opportunities.

Paterson was a happy ward and that was good for the
morale of the patients. Phyllida was very impressed by
the courage that most of them showed, coming in for
major surgery and dreading the results in many cases,
but managing to laugh and make jokes and rally each
other and even flirt with the doctors and put on a brave

face for visitors along with the indispensable lipstick and pretty nightdress or bed-jacket.

She hurried along the corridor towards the ward and cut the corner in her usual fashion. The unexpected collision with Ross Harman, doing exactly the same thing on his way from the ward, knocked all the breath from her body and his broad shoulder, just level with her head, sent her cap flying to the floor.

'Oh, I'm sorry . . . !' It was an automatic reflex for accident-prone Phyllida to apologise, even when she wasn't to blame.

He steadied her with both hands on the neat waist and there was the hint of laughter in the depths of the dark eyes. 'All right, Nurse? Sorry about that! My fault!'

'My cap!' she exclaimed, halfway between amusement and exasperation.

Ross smiled. 'It does seem to have a life of its own.' He bent to retrieve it and handed it to her with a flourish. 'I daresay Matron used to have the same problem with her cap when she was a junior,' he said comfortingly.

Phyllida was not comforted. She didn't think that Matron had ever been a junior! Or she would have more sympathy with the scrapes that she fell into with monotonous regularity.

She sighed. 'Wretched thing! Now I shall have to wrestle with it all over again and I'm running out of hairpins. And time! I hope you've sweetened Georgy Knight's temper with your well-known charm!'

He cocked an eyebrow at the impulsive words, amused. 'Well, I did try,' he drawled. 'Just to prove that registrars do have their uses.'

As she smiled, Ross discovered that she was a pretty girl with that glint of gold in her hair and the deep blue eyes that met his own without coquetry. He did not usually pursue the first-years. They were too young and took things too seriously and Matron strongly disapproved of doctors who broke the hearts of her young nurses. He was a very sensual man who didn't hesitate to make the most of any opportunity that came his way, but he steered clear of innocents like this one. He had noticed her about the ward, of course. Juniors who were frequently read the riot act by irate sister or staff nurse were not easily overlooked on any ward, he thought dryly.

She hurried away, cap in hand, starched skirts rustling. Ross looked after her, thoughtful. The traditional blue dress of a first-year, with its short puffed sleeves and matching belt, suited that slender figure. He admired the tiny waist and trim hips and the legs that managed to look very shapely for all the regulation black stockings and flat-heeled black brogues. He had noticed the tempting tilt of firm young breasts beneath the crisp apron front. He was not the kind of man to miss an attractive detail of that nature.

Georgy was playing hard to get and the latest rebuff was rankling. He was tempted to punish her with a little flirtation with the junior nurse from her ward. He was tempted for its own sake, too . . .

Phyllida pushed open the swing doors of the ward rather more cautiously than usual, her cap fixed so firmly in position that her head felt as though it bristled with hairpins.

Georgy Knight looked up from the desk where she

was adding a few lines to the Report. 'Where on earth have you been, Nurse Sims?'

'I'm sorry, Staff. I've been having trouble with my cap.' She didn't mean to mention that brief encounter with Ross Harman. The staff nurse would only assume that it had been engineered. She wanted the registrar for herself and she kept a jealous eye on any possible rival.

'Go and help Nurse Buckley with the dressings—and don't think you're getting away with being late this time! Your name is down on Matron's Report. Sister is far too lax with you, in my opinion!'

'Yes, Staff.' Phyllida was too used to the sharp note in the older girl's voice to take much notice of it.

She hurried down the ward to help the overworked third-year nurse who had to contend with autocratic Georgy Knight as well as the inexperience and ineptitude of the first-years. It was to her credit that she took it all in her stride and remained on friendly terms with senior and junior staff.

Dressings was a routine chore that took a lot of time and gentle hands, but provided a nurse with a valuable opportunity for getting to know the patients on a busy ward. Helen Buckley was grateful for some assistance and she valued the first-year as the staff nurse did not. She welcomed her with a warm smile, knowing that Phyllida had a gift for putting patients at ease and the most sensitive and careful of hands for all her notable clumsiness.

Helen agreed with Sister Hamilton that it was mostly due to the impetuosity of youth and the dash of eagerness. Time and experience would cure both. The junior simply wanted to do too many things at once to prove her worth on the ward. Given a set task, she settled and concentrated and did it capably and well, forgetting to be clumsy or awkward.

The patients liked her and missed her when she was off duty for she had a warmth of heart and a genuine interest and a sweet nature that shone from the blue eyes and the swift, spontaneous smile. An elderly German patient who had fled her native land and its alien politics in the thirties and never quite mastered the finer points of the English language, had taken a fancy to Phyllida and called her the 'nicely nurse'. The nickname amused the medical students and it had stuck—and she *was* a nicely nurse, Helen thought, noticing that her junior smiled and chatted warmly and reassuringly to the patient while she assisted with the dressing. In fact, Phyllida was a nice girl who got on well with everyone— except Georgy Knight who seemed to have a down on her for no reason at all.

Wearing a mask to guard against cross-infection, Helen carefully exposed the wound, removing the dirty dressing with forceps and placing it in a disposal bag. With a sterile swab dipped in antiseptic lotion, she cleaned the wound and covered it with a clean dressing.

Mrs Schwodler had undergone surgery for a bowel cancer. She was not doing very well after a partial coleostomy and Professor Wilson had reluctantly decided on further and more drastic surgery. He had detailed his registrar to break the news to the patient that morning.

Now Mrs Schwodler confided in Phyllida, clinging to her hand, crying a little. Senior Sister Tutor of the PTS warned each new set of student nurses against becoming emotionally involved with patients. But Phyllida had grown fond of the gentle old lady who tried so hard not to give any trouble and she sympathised with her fear and anxiety. There was the hint of tears in her own eyes, but she talked brightly and cheerfully of better days to come after the operation, of a speedy convalescence, of the patient's return to her daughter's home in the very near future.

It was part of a nurse's rôle to cheer and comfort and reassure without making a patient feel that she was hardened to suffering and mental anguish. Listening as she carefully strapped the dressing in place, Helen thought that the kind-hearted junior struck just the right note.

She straightened, removed her mask. 'Make Mrs Schwodler comfortable and clear away the trolley while I make a start with Mrs Eliot. Then lay up a fresh trolley for Miss Munro's dressing, please, Nurse.'

Phyllida nodded. Helen was a dear, she thought warmly. It was like her to realise that the old lady was too distressed to be left abruptly in mid-air. Unlike Georgy Knight, *she* did not think that routine chores came before the patient's mental and emotional needs.

She settled Mrs Schwodler while telling her all about the grandmother who had undergone the same kind of surgery and never looked back. She was rewarded when the old lady began to accept the idea of further surgery with a degree of resignation and a flicker of hope for the future.

Phillida took the trolley back to the clinical room and cleared it, carefully putting used instruments in the tray that stood ready to go into the steriliser. Then she began to lay up a trolley for the next dressing. She was just taking a sterile surgical pack from a drawer when she heard a familiar voice in the corridor and she moved to the open door on an impulse. 'Mr Harman . . . !'

He turned, surprised. They might speak at a chance encounter, but it was not usual for first-year nurses to approach senior registrars on or off the ward. It was against all the rules of hospital etiquette, in fact. 'Yes?'

'May I speak to you? Can you spare a moment?'

He raised an eyebrow. He nodded to his equally surprised colleague, the Professor's houseman. 'Have a look at those X-rays and let me know what you think . . .' He strolled towards the junior nurse who waited by the door of the clinical room, apparently unaware of the enormity of claiming his attention in that very confident manner. 'What can I do for you, Nurse?' There was a faint twinkle in the dark eyes.

Phyllida came straight to the point. 'It's Mrs Schwodler. She's dreading another operation. I know it must be necessary. But will she be all right—*really* all right? It seems dreadful to put her through such an ordeal, mental and physical, if she isn't going to *do!*' She used the hospital term for patients who were expected to make a complete recovery from illness or surgery.

Ross tugged at his ear, a habitual gesture when he was briefly at a loss. It was a frontal assault, demanding answer. He wished he knew the answer. To the young, everything was black and white, he thought wryly. They didn't care for the grey areas of compromise.

'She'll die if we don't operate,' he said quietly. 'Not too soon, perhaps—but very painfully. This way she gets a fighting chance.'

'I see.' Phyllida bit her lip. 'Thanks. You didn't mind that I asked you?'

He smiled. 'Not at all. Fond of the old lady, are you? Don't get too attached to patients if you can help it, Nurse. It clouds the judgment.'

'I *can't* help it,' she said firmly. 'Isn't caring what nursing is all about? Everyone says that you're a good surgeon. Doesn't that mean that you care about people, too?'

He looked down at her steadily. She was impulsive, idealistic. But all heart, he thought, warming to her. This girl was more than just a pretty face. She had a great deal of character.

'A surgeon has to be caring *and* detached,' he told her carefully. He saw argument leap into the very blue eyes. 'Look, there isn't time to discuss it here and now,' he added hastily. 'Why don't we meet for a drink this evening?'

Phyllida didn't hesitate. 'Yes. All right. I'm on duty until eight. Can you make it nine o'clock?'

'Nine o'clock,' he agreed. 'In the Kingfisher.'

Ross pushed his way into the ward where the house-man was waiting for him. He was amused and rather intrigued by that ready acceptance of his invitation. Didn't she know that she was playing with fire? Didn't she realise that most of the juniors at Hartlake would be green with envy? He suspected that the youthful Nurse Sims didn't even see him as a very attractive man. He was just a surgeon who seemed to hold the power of life or death in his trained hands . . .

Phyllida discovered that her heart was thudding un-evenly against her ribs. She had been so concerned for

Mrs Schwodler that she hadn't hesitated to fly in the face of etiquette. It had been nice of him to answer her question so patiently. Nicer still that he had smiled in that understanding way and cautioned her gently about the dangers of caring too much. And she liked the easy friendliness with which he had thrown out that casual invitation, making it so easy for her to accept.

Perhaps it was seeing him every day on the ward. Perhaps it was the warmth of his smile and the disarming, very charming manner. But Phyllida found it easy to like him. She had no qualms about meeting him that evening. He might be a rake, but she suspected that girls had always thrown themselves at that very good-looking head.

She didn't see why a girl couldn't be just friends even with a reputed Casanova if she made it clear from the start that she wasn't the type to sleep around. She was sure that she could trust him. She didn't blame any man for taking what was offered to him on a plate. She just didn't mean to offer anything more than a friendly and undemanding relationship!

She trundled the trolley into the ward and began to make her way towards Miss Munro's bed. Halfway there, she saw that she had forgotten the antiseptic lotion. She hurried away to get it from the clinical room—and turned, horrified, as the Professor came out of a side room, deep in discussion with the staff nurse, and collided with the abandoned trolley. Phyllida hadn't even known that he was on the ward, doing his round with his registrar and houseman.

She flew to apologise, banners of dismay flying in her cheeks. Georgy Knight glared so fiercely that she saw her name on Matron's report in scarlet letters ten-feet high. The Professor looked down his nose at a careless junior. The houseman entered a note in the patient's medical file, carefully not looking at anyone. Ross Harman met Phyllida's rueful eyes and shook his head at her in amused reproach.

'Remove that trolley at once!' Georgy Knight snapped. 'And I'll speak to you later, Nurse Sims,' she added ominously.

It was one of those days, Phyllida sighed as she took the trolley back to the clinical room and collected the lotion. She would be jumping through hoops for the staff nurse for the rest of the day, she knew.

The only bright spot was her date with Ross Harman—and that seemed a million light years away!

CHAPTER TWO

PHYLLIDA's heart was fluttering as she left the Nurses' Home, irreverently known as The Nunnery to medical students, and crossed the busy High Street to meet Ross Harman in the Kingfisher. It had seemed both right and natural that he should issue that friendly invitation and she should accept it—at the time. Suddenly she was not so sure that it was a good idea to spend what was left of the evening in his company.

He was a registrar and she was only a first-year. Hospital rules and regulations decreed that never the twain should meet except in the course of their work. If they did meet then it was wise to be out of sight and sound of Hartlake. For the grapevine was very efficient and Matron frowned on personal relationships between senior and junior members of staff. It was usually the girl who was scolded for neglecting her studies and risking the good name of a Hartlake nurse and threatened with dismissal if she continued to flout the rules.

Phyllida had scarcely exchanged two words with Ross Harman until that day, on or off the ward. They might find that they had nothing to say to each other. She might discover that she didn't like him, after all. He might be very bored.

She was nothing like the girls he usually dated. Georgy Knight, for instance. Georgy was lovely with her pale blonde hair and sparkling grey eyes and classic good looks—and she probably didn't treat her boy-friends to a taste of that famous temper! She was eye-catching and glamorous and she seemed to know all the answers. Just Ross Harman's type, in fact.

Phyllida was a little wary of Ross Harman's type and inclined to be distrustful of most men. She watched other girls falling in and out of love as though it was a delightful game and thought that few men could be trusted to play it according to the rules. It seemed to Phyllida that most of them took what they wanted with little regard for the girls or for the consequences. Remembering her sister, pregnant and left to get on with it at seventeen, Phyllida knew all about consequences.

She was a virgin and she wanted to stay that way until she married. Or until she fell deeply and lastingly in love with a man who felt the same way about her, anyway.

Meanwhile, men were amusing companions, useful escorts, even good friends, but nothing more. She was not a flirt and she didn't encourage men to care too much or expect too much. Most of her friends at Hartlake were medical students. One or two were housemen. A registrar was flying high—and perhaps dangerously, remembering his reputation!

A little apprehensive, she went into the pub, looked around. It was a popular haunt of Hartlake staff and it was crowded that night. Phyllida felt a foolish panic that she wouldn't find him in the crush—or, more likely, that he wouldn't recognise her out of uniform.

Ross saw her enter, hesitate, look around the big, crowded room with a slight uncertainty. Then, catching sight of him, her smile was so swift and spontaneous with a delight that he didn't recognise as relief that he was suddenly wary.

The last thing he wanted was a first-year believing herself in love with him. A man like himself was better off spending his leisure hours with the Georgys of this world. He was twenty-eight and there had been a lot of women in his life and not one of them had meant much—and that was the way he liked it. He valued his freedom. He didn't have time for love and happy ever after while his work and his ambitions took most of his energies and enthusiasm.

Phyllida saw that his eyes were guarded as he greeted her and settled her in the corner seat. She could kick herself for the eager way she had smiled and hurried over to him. She had almost fallen on his neck with gratitude for being there, she thought wryly, furious with herself for such naive behaviour. No wonder there was a slight coolness in his manner.

'What do you like to drink?'

Phyllida hesitated. She knew that he would be keeping her at a safe distance for the rest of the evening. She wouldn't have to worry about fighting him off! Even so . . . 'Just a tomato juice,' she said lightly. A girl needed all her wits about her when dealing with a rake.

'Have a vodka with it,' he suggested.

'No, thanks . . . really!' She smiled at him, not too warmly.

She studied him while he stood at the bar. In the formal dark suit, he was impressive among the crowd in their jeans and T-shirts and sweaters. Tall, broad-shouldered, with the athletic build of the rugger player, he was an attractive man. Crisp dark hair curled about the temples and on the nape of his neck, fell across the handsome brow. His lean, good-looking face had a hint of summer tan. The dark, deep-set eyes always seemed to have a glimmer of a smile in their depths.

Ross brought her tomato juice and another ice-cold lager for himself and sat down. She smiled at him with a hint of shyness. He smiled, reassuring. She sipped her soft drink. He reached for his beer. She was a pretty girl, but she seemed to have nothing to say for herself. Ross wondered wryly how he came to be spending hard-earned free time with an unwordly junior nurse. He thought with sudden longing of the delectable Georgy, out with someone else that evening.

Phyllida's restless fingers toyed with the pleats of her skirt. She needn't have bothered to put on the daffodil silk dress and matching jacket in his honour, she thought ruefully. Actually, she was just a little over-dressed for a quiet drink in the pub. She might have been more at her ease if she had kept on her uniform. Hartlake was common ground, after all. They probably had nothing else in common . . .

'Did you get through the day without any more disasters?' Ross asked, a twinkle in his dark eyes. 'You damaged the Professor's dignity this morning, you know!'

Phyllida laughed. 'I could give a crash course in how to lose friends and alienate staff nurses! And I do mean *crash* course! Some days it seems that everything I touch goes wrong.' She sighed. 'I expect you think I'm a dreadful nurse.'

'You do seem to cause chaos without even trying,' he agreed, gently teasing.

'*Et tu, Brute . . .*'

Ross smiled. 'Did it sound like a reproach? Sorry! I expect you hear too many of those.' He hesitated. 'Georgy Knight is a little hard on you, isn't she?' He wondered if she knew that he had been trying for some time to lure Georgy from the arms of one of his colleagues.

'She's a marvellous nurse and a terrific teacher,' she said generously, meaning it. 'You wouldn't believe how patient she can be if she thinks someone is really trying! She just doesn't suffer fools gladly, that's all—and I'm the Paterson jester with bells on! I'm twice as bad when she's breathing down my neck, of course. Sister tells me to do something and leaves me to get on with it—and only comes running when she hears the inevitable crash!' she added with a rueful laugh.

'But you like nursing?'

'Oh, yes!' She coloured slightly as his smile deepened, crinkling the dark eyes. She must sound absurdly young and eager, she thought. But she did like nursing and why should she pretend to be blasé and wordly-wise when she was nothing of the kind? 'I just hope that I'll manage to get my SRN before Hartlake crashes about my ears,' she added, keeping it light.

'I'm sure you will. It's survived a good many juniors for a very long time.' He indicated her empty glass. 'Another drink? Have something stronger this time,' he suggested.

'Not just now. Later, perhaps.' Even as she spoke, Phyllida wondered if she was taking too much for granted. There might not be any 'later' as far as he was concerned. He might have decided to buy her one more drink and then produce a tactful reason for making his escape. It was hard to believe that he was enjoying her company.

'I don't suppose you had time to eat? I thought we'd have a meal at the new Italian restaurant in Arnott Place,' he said lightly.

He might almost have read her mind. Phyllida brightened. 'I'd like that,' she said warmly. 'But I have to be in by twelve. I haven't a late pass.'

First-years were required to live in unless they had a family home within easy reach of Hartlake and one of the drawbacks to the Nurses' Home was Sister Vernon who kept a vigilant eye on their comings and goings. She saw herself as a substitute mother to her young charges and that could be irksome. For some of the student nurses had come into nursing to escape parental supervision.

'Isn't there a ground-floor window with a conveniently faulty catch that's been used by naughty nurses since time immemorial?'

Phyllida smiled. 'I daresay you've pushed a few girls through it in your time!'

'In my medical student days, I managed to persuade one or two juniors to be naughty, I must admit,' he said, eyes dancing. 'It's a long time ago, but I haven't lost all my powers of persuasion, I hope.'

'With my luck, I'd be caught and I'm in quite enough trouble,' she demurred. 'Matron has a list of my disasters to lecture me about in the morning.'

'Then I'll take care to return you to your ivory tower by midnight.'

'*Discreetly*,' she said dryly. 'I don't want the whole of

Hartlake knowing that I've been out with you!' Her eyes teased him. 'You do have a certain reputation!'

Ross raised an amused eyebrow. 'At the moment, I suppose you're invisible?' he suggested, sardonic. 'Tongues are probably already wagging and I expect Matron will have a full report of all that happens on her desk before dawn!'

'That should make dull reading,' she said lightly. 'Nothing's going to happen!'

He smiled into the blue eyes with their unmistakable warning. 'It might . . .' There was more teasing than promise behind the words.

'It won't!' she said, very firmly.

He laughed softly and touched her cheek in a light, almost caress. 'Of course not,' he agreed, reassuring her. 'I don't always live up to my reputation. I do have the occasional night off from seducing pretty nurses.'

There was something so dismissive in that light touch and the even lighter words that Phyllida felt a flicker of disappointment. She was careful not to let it show.

She liked the food and the atmosphere of the intimate restaurant that was probably much too expensive for her own slender purse. She liked his company, too. She drew him to talk about his work and his ambitions and she was fascinated by all that he told her. She was impressed by his confidence, too. He was working to-wards a surgical consultancy and she didn't doubt that he would get it. Everyone said that he was a very good surgeon. Listening to him, it seemed to Phyllida that he was also a very caring man although he claimed to have a detached attitude to his patients.

He smiled, broke off suddenly. 'That's enough about

me,' he said firmly. 'Talking shop to a pretty girl is no way to spend an evening.'

'Well, I enjoy it. Juniors don't get much insight into the real world of surgery,' she told him. 'It seems to be all back rubs and bedpans as far as we're concerned!'

'Where would the patients be without you?' he comforted. 'Or the doctors! Paterson is a much brighter ward since you began to work on it, you know.'

She looked at him with sceptical amusement. 'More eventful, anyway,' she said dryly. 'People never know whether to duck or dodge or dive under the nearest bed every time I come on the ward.'

Ross laughed, delighted with the engaging readiness to laugh at her disastrous progress through training. He liked her. He liked the way she listened so attentively and with such genuine interest and asked intelligent and perceptive questions. He liked her quick understanding of his dedication and his ambition to make a name for himself as a consultant.

He liked her smile, too. It dawned in the lovely eyes before it curved her lips and illumined that pretty face to real and effective beauty. He liked the warm and generous personality and the hint of touch-me-not that was so rare in the girls that he usually dated.

It was a pleasant evening. Ross was relieved to realise that the eager delight of her greeting had been due to friendliness rather than an unwelcome degree of involvement. Far from being a mistake, taking her out had turned into a success, he decided.

Her failure to flirt made him feel that liking and mutual interests and enjoyment of each other's company might be an excellent foundation for a lasting friendship.

He had always scoffed at the ideal of a platonic relationship between man and woman. Now he saw it as a very real possibility. A man could tire of the pursuit of sexual conquest and it was good to relax with a girl who obviously did not want or expect lovemaking to round off the evening.

True to his word, he took her back to the Nurses' Home with minutes to spare before the main door was closed against latecomers who would have to ring the night bell and explain themselves to a disapproving Sister Vernon.

There was a flurry of nurses arriving to sign in and hurry to their beds. Most of them might think it an archaic system, but few of them chose to flout it.

Ross and Phyllida paused briefly in the shadows a few yards from the tall building that was part of the sprawling complex of the world-famous hospital.

Phyllida looked up at the registrar, tall and much too attractive in the muted street lighting, and as remote as any stranger. With a sinking of her heart, she knew that he wasn't even going to kiss her. It didn't say much for her feminine attractions that a notorious rake could take her out and scarcely reach out for her hand during the entire evening, she thought ruefully.

'I'd better go in,' she said, rather lamely.

'Yes.' Ross was tempted to put an arm about the slender waist and kiss the uplifted face with its slightly anxious expression. She was very sweet and rather appealing. But he did not care for the fact that other couples in the shadows were saying their goodnights in similar fashion To make even the lightest of amorous overtures would possibly cheapen a promising relationship, he felt. He smiled and touched her cheek in that half-caress. 'Don't create too much mayhem on the ward in the morning, will you?'

Phyllida heaved a mock sigh. 'What it is to have a reputation!'

He laughed. 'I know the feeling . . .'

She watched him walk away, striding along the pavement as though he was glad to put distance between them. Had he been so bored, so disappointed in the evening? She was not at all his type, of course, she reminded herself, facing facts. She was much too young, too gauche, too inexperienced.

Having made a date with her on a sudden and probably regretted impulse, he had made the best of it and tried to give her a good time. But she could not convince herself that he had enjoyed it. After all, there had not even been a hint of another meeting away from the ward.

It was most unlike the level-headed and usually light-hearted Phyllida to feel so depressed as she got into bed and drew the covers over her head, shutting out the light and the excited chatter of her flatmate. Kate had spent the evening with a houseman and wanted to talk about it at great length.

'I'm asleep,' she said, muffled, when Kate asked for the third time if she was listening and at last her friend took the hint.

Phyllida tried to sleep but she found that the image of Ross Harman was etched so vividly on her mind's eye that he threatened to disturb her dreams. She tried not to remember the way her heart had jolted at the touch of his hand on her cheek, the smile in his dark eyes. She must not like him too much, she told herself firmly . . .

And knew, when he walked into the ward the following morning, that it was rather too late for such good advice. She already liked him more than was wise in view of his reputation for light and meaningless loving.

She saw the way that he smiled at Georgy Knight and felt a foolish pang. He smiled at most women in just that way, of course. It was part of his stock in trade as a rake, no doubt. Any girl would be a fool to believe that he meant it.

Remembering how he had talked about his work and his hopes and plans for the future, Phyllida felt sure that the attractive Ross Harman didn't mean to expend time and energy on falling in love with any girl. There were many doctors at Hartlake who felt the same way, she knew, avoiding serious involvement with the girls they dated. She reminded herself that his motto seemed to be 'safety in numbers' for there had been an awful lot of girls in his life if the grapevine was to be believed. It would be very foolish to allow herself to care too much for such a man.

But she did like him, she thought wistfully. He stirred feelings that no other man had ever evoked, too. Something within her seemed to respond to his merest touch. She ached for his arms about her and the warmth of his lips on her own—and it hurt to know that it was never likely to happen. For hadn't he shown that she wasn't at all attractive to him in that way? Wasn't it obvious that he wouldn't ask her to go out with him again?

Foolish tears pricked suddenly behind her eyes and she hastily bent her head over the patient's chart. She entered a rather blurred temperature reading and returned the chart to its place at the foot of the bed. It fell to the floor with a loud clatter. Phyllida had failed to hook it properly over the bed-rail.

She could almost hear the exasperated sigh of the much-tried Sister Hamilton from the other end of the ward as she accompanied the registrar on his morning round. Knowing that all eyes were on her, Phyllida blushed hotly. Without even looking at him, she knew that Ross Harman's dark eyes were twinkling with amusement.

Scarlet, she picked up the chart and put it very carefully over the bed-rail before she moved on to the next patient. As she reached for the clinical thermometer in its container above the bed, Mrs Liblitz smiled at her in sympathy.

She was an enormously fat and jolly woman who laughed her way through life despite the diabetic condition that had led to the loss of a leg. The life and soul of the ward, she never minded what she said to anyone if it raised a laugh. But she had a kind heart and she felt for the embarrassed young nurse who seemed to be perpetually in trouble.

Heaving herself upright against the pillows, Mrs Liblitz clutched unthinkingly at Phyllida's arm. Taken by surprise, she dropped the thermometer and heard it break at her feet. It was the second that week, but this time it really wasn't her fault. However, Sister would scold and point out that she must always be prepared for such an eventuality.

As she hurried for brush and pan to clear away the broken glass and mercury, she passed a bed where a houseman was setting up an intravenous drip of Hart-

man's solution for a patient who was due to go to
Theatres that morning.

Kevin Lawson grinned at her. 'Not bad for an encore,'
he said softly. 'What can we expect for a grand finale?'

Phyllida paused. She smiled, a trifle wryly, too used to
being teased about her mishaps to take exception to it.
'Why did I come into nursing?' she sighed. 'There must
be easier ways to earn a living.' She pretended an
interest in what he was doing with the length of tubing.

'I daresay you like to live dangerously.' He adjusted
the clamp with experienced hands to achieve a regular
flow of the solution through the drip. 'But I think Sister's
on the edge of a nervous breakdown, poor woman.'
Seeing Sister cross the ward towards them even as he
spoke, he added hastily: 'If you could just pass me that
air-inlet filter, Nurse . . .'

'You should inform me if you require someone to
assist you, Dr Lawson,' Sister said frostily. 'I'm afraid
that Nurse Sims is very busy just now. Please clear up
that mess and then get on with the temperature round,
Nurse . . . as soon as possible!'

'Yes, Sister . . .'

Phyllida went on her way, slightly chastened, while
Kevin promptly assured Sister in his meekest tone that
he could manage very well and wouldn't require any of
her very busy nurses to help him.

Georgy Knight was doing the drugs round with
another nurse to check each dosage as she measured out
medicine or counted out tablets after checking the
patient's chart.

As Phyllida drew level with the drugs trolley, the staff
nurse threw her a very venomous glance. 'You do draw

attention to yourself, don't you? Usually when there's a doctor or two on the ward, I've noticed!' she said acidly.

Phyllida didn't answer. There was no point in trying to defend herself against the unfair accusation. The senior nurse was determined not to like her at the best of times. If she had heard through the too-efficient grapevine that Ross Harman had taken her out on the previous evening then it explained the greater degree of dislike behind the words.

Georgy was a very efficient nurse who always seemed to know exactly what to do in any situation. But she lacked warmth in her dealings with the patients and her fellow-nurses. Until Ross Harman walked into the ward. Then she became sparkling and vibrant and so pleasant to almost everyone that her change of attitude was rapidly becoming a joke among the juniors—as long as she wasn't about to hear them discussing her interest in the registrar!

The staff nurse obviously had a soft spot for Ross Harman. Phyllida wished it wasn't so obvious that he had a soft spot for her, too. She thought that he sometimes came into the ward only to snatch an opportunity for a few words with Georgy and his work provided plenty of excuses.

Georgy was very lovely, of course . . .

CHAPTER THREE

Ross walked out of the ward as she approached the swing doors. He walked briskly, coat flying, passing her without so much as a smile.

Phyllida looked after him, knowing it was foolish to feel hurt. Registrars were very busy men with much on their minds and he had no reason to snub her. He was probably hurrying to an emergency. Or he was due in Theatres and had been delayed on the ward and still had to scrub-up.

He always seemed to have time to smile at Georgy Knight, Phyllida thought with a stir of jealous resentment. But she was just a very junior nurse and no doubt one looked much like another to a doctor in a hurry . . .

Sister supplied a new thermometer without the scold that Phyllida had been expecting. There was resignation rather than irritation in the quiet voice as she said: 'You will try to be more careful, won't you, Nurse Sims? I know that juniors always feel that there isn't enough time for all the work, but you must learn to hurry without haste. You can't expect the patients to have confidence in a nurse who is constantly dropping or forgetting things.'

'No, Sister. I'm sorry, Sister. I will try,' Phyllida said earnestly.

Sister Hamilton's eyes softened as they rested on the girl's rueful face. She had a sneaking sympathy with this particular junior who reminded her of what she had been at the same age . . . not as clumsy, perhaps, but certainly prone to doing all the wrong things in her eagerness to prove that she was an asset to the ward.

In those days, Sister Booth had been in charge of Paterson. Now retired, her sharp tongue was still remembered by those who had incurred her displeasure. She had run the ward with an iron discipline, maybe old-fashioned but certainly effective, and even the most autocratic of senior consultants had bowed to her ruling, respecting her judgment and experience.

Things had changed at Hartlake—and not always for the better, Sister Hamilton mused. Junior nurses were no longer so eager to obey, so reluctant to question or so overawed by authority when they began their training and they did not easily accept that rules and regulations were not just hidebound traditions but necessary for the smooth running of a very big hospital with its many patients and staff.

'Very well, Nurse. Carry on . . .'

'Thank you, Sister.'

Phyllida returned to the temperature round, taking such pains to be careful that it took her almost twice as long as it should and an impatient Georgy Knight told her off for dawdling.

Later that morning, she was tidying the big linen cupboard with its plastic packs of laundered sheets when Kevin Lawson paused by the open door and looked in. 'Found a safe place for you, have they?' he said lightly.

Phyllida, her head full of a very different doctor, was startled out of a reverie by the sound of his voice. She turned, smiled at him. 'I guess you haven't seen me surrounded by a few dozen plastic packs that slide off the shelves as soon as they see me coming,' she joked.

He was a good-looking young man, so blond that his colleagues jokingly referred to him as Sir Lionel's white-headed boy. Clever and able, with a great deal of promise, he had an engaging smile and a degree of charm that made him popular with the juniors.

His grey eyes appraised Phyllida with warm approval as he laughed at the ready retort. Even a very busy houseman could find time to notice someone as pretty and as appealing as this particular first-year nurse. 'I've tickets for the Rugger Club dance on Saturday,' he said. 'How about coming with me?'

Still smarting slightly from Ross Harman's casual attitude, even though she knew the demands that made it difficult for personal relationships to take priority over his work, Phyllida accepted the invitation. She liked the houseman's easy friendliness and she certainly didn't mean to stay in every night and dream of the unattainable, she told herself firmly.

Kevin went away, pleased, and Phyllida finished the tidying of the linen cupboard and then went to ask Sister what she should do next. Sister was taking her coffee break in her sitting-room and Georgy Knight was at the ward desk, talking to Ross Harman.

Phyllida waited, hands demurely behind her back, trying not to hear any of a conversation that did not appear to have much to do with medicine.

He had obviously come to the ward from Theatres with special instructions for a patient's after-care for he still wore the thin green cap over his unruly dark hair, green trousers and smock and surgical boots. His green mask was lying loosely about his neck by its ties.

Suddenly aware of Phyllida, Ross broke off in the middle of his persuasions. He had been in hot pursuit of the staff nurse for some time and felt that he was getting somewhere at last. She was rather more encouraging than usual.

He glanced at the junior, standing so correctly and slightly to the side of the desk, carefully not appearing to look or listen, and there was the hint of a smile in his eyes. He liked Phyllida and he had enjoyed their evening and he meant to take her out again. But for the moment, he was far from ready to forgo all that the lovely Georgy promised.

Georgy turned to the girl, impatient. 'What is it, Nurse?'

'What would you like me to do now, please, Staff?'

Georgy looked thoughtful. 'Have you had your break?'

'Not yet, Staff.' Phyllida wouldn't look at the registrar although she knew that his dark eyes were looking at her. She didn't want him to think that he was anything more to her than just a man who had taken her out for a drink and a meal—and she was afraid that her own eyes might betray that she liked him too much for comfort.

'Mrs Ellison has come back from Theatres and she's due for a half-hourly p.t.r., so you can do that and then take your break. Don't forget to aspirate her, by the way.'

'Yes, Staff. Thank you, Staff . . .'

Mrs Ellison was sleeping off the effects of the anaesthetic after the removal of her gall-bladder. She had been taken to the recovery room immediately after the operation and roused by a persistent theatre nurse and then allowed to slip back into sleep before being finally returned to the ward.

She was reluctant to wake and was very drowsy as Phyllida took her temperature and checked her respiration and asked her how she was feeling. She took her pulse and then drew off the contents of the stomach tube.

Then she wrapped the wide bandage about Mrs Ellison's upper arm and squeezed the rubber bulb of the sphygmomanometer, watching the rising level. She listened to the systolic murmur with the stethoscope and made a note of the reading on the patient's chart. Mrs Ellison had already drifted back into sleep.

She was so intent on her task that she wasn't aware of Ross, watching from the doorway, until he spoke.

'Florence Nightingale, I presume?' he said lightly. Startled, Phyllida turned. 'Any problems?' He came further into the room.

'None at all.' She bent her head over the chart. Ross looked over her shoulder to read the figures, so close that her heart quickened with a very foolish excitement.

'How's the blood pressure?'

'Normal reading.'

He nodded. 'Good.' He was very conscious of her femininity, the perfume of her hair teasing his senses, the nearness of her evoking a sharp and totally unexpected ache of desire. 'You're sending mine sky-high,' he said softly, impulsively.

Phyllida moved away hastily. 'Save it for Georgy Knight!' she said quickly—and could have bitten off that betraying tongue as he raised an amused eyebrow.

'Do I detect a hint of jealousy?' he drawled, teasing, dark eyes dancing.

Phyllida laughed. 'The conceit of the man!' she declared brightly. 'I merely meant that you're wasting your efforts on me. I'm not interested.'

Ross studied her with that disarming smile playing about his sensual mouth. 'I refuse to believe that you're cold. I think you're just cautious.'

'With good reason where you're concerned, don't you think?' she countered swiftly.

'My reputation? I'm a rake and no innocent girl is safe at my hands?' His smile deepened. 'If you really thought that, you wouldn't have met me last night. You didn't come to any harm, did you?'

A little colour stole into her face as she recalled her disappointment that he hadn't even tried to kiss her. 'That's true, but—'

'I didn't want you?' he broke in swiftly, reading her mind with disconcerting ease. 'Is that what you thought? Just because I don't do my kissing in public?' His gaze rested on her flushed face with a little amused tenderness. 'Silly girl . . .'

Phyllida felt her heart turn over as she met the melting warmth in his eyes. She didn't know what to believe. He had certainly seemed uninterested and although it had been a relief in one way it had also been a humiliation.

Now, the unexpected overture was not entirely welcome because she fancied he was an instinctive flirt who spoke and acted according to the mood of the moment. And perhaps he had sensed that unwilling response in her to his nearness. Phyllida realised that he was not the kind of man to overlook even the smallest opportunity for light-hearted flirtation. It would be a mistake to take him seriously, she reminded herself again.

'Don't spoil things, Ross,' she said, very carefully. 'Don't drag sex into a very ordinary relationship. Can't we just be friends?'

'Any way you want it,' he said lightly.

Her heart sank. He had taken her words for the rebuff that it undeniably was, but she hadn't meant to sound quite so final. Now she had the dreadful feeling that he wouldn't bother with her again. For men like Ross Harman couldn't help bringing sex into every affair, however trivial—and if he didn't get what he wanted from one girl there were plenty of other girls. And Georgy Knight was probably only too willing to melt into his arms.

Sister's distinctive voice was heard in the corridor outside the side ward and Ross moved towards the door. She heard him speak to Sister and then he left the ward. Phyllida turned back to Mrs Ellison, wondering if the woman had heard any of that brief and very unprofessional exchange.

She checked the drip and the drainage tube and found everything in correct order. Then she made her way to the juniors' room and made herself a cup of coffee and went over and over that encounter with Ross in her mind, convinced that she had said all the wrong things.

Phyllida knew it would be much too easy to like him more than was wise, remembering not only his reputation but also the dedication to his work which would probably come before any woman for a very long time. Only a fool would fall in love with a registrar who was not only rakish but ambitious!

While she worked on Paterson, she was bound to see a great deal of him. But she didn't have to meet him off the ward. She didn't have to waste time and energy in dreaming about him. She didn't have to behave as though there were no other men in the world but Ross Harman.

At nineteen, Phyllida was more mature and more level-headed than many girls of that age. She knew that Ross had come dangerously near to charming her heart into his keeping without even trying—and he hadn't even kissed her!

She didn't think that he would ask her for another date. But if he did, she would turn him down. If she did go out with him, she would keep him at a safe distance. They might be friends after a fashion but he would be disappointed if he had hopes that they would ever be lovers, she told herself firmly . . .

Ross was in and out of the ward during most of the day. It wasn't difficult to avoid him, for registrars and first-years had very little to do with each other in the course of their work. And Georgy Knight seemed to be ensuring that she was busy with routine chores in sluice or ward kitchen or sent off the ward on an errand whenever Ross Harman was around, Phyllida decided.

Being a conscientious girl who really wanted to qualify as a state registered nurse in the fullness of time, Phyllida spent the next two evenings with her books.

She refused to be tempted into going to a party with Patti and Kate, her friends and flatmates. Jacqui, her remaining flatmate, went to the cinema with a girl-friend. Phyllida was quite content to be on her own with her textbooks and notebooks. In fact, she welcomed the chance to study without distraction.

When she eventually put her books aside, feeling as though her brain was stuffed full of facts, she picked up a little frock she was smocking for her sister's baby, Amy. The hands that could at times be so awkward and clumsy when she most wanted to do well were skilled at needlework and her friends admired the exquisite embroidery that was a kind of relaxation for Phyllida.

Unfortunately, although her hands were busily occupied, her thoughts were free to wander where they would. Just lately, they turned much too frequently to Ross Harman and that was ridiculous when she scarcely knew him, she scolded herself.

Since she had rebuffed him in the side ward, he had not tried to see or speak to her. The grapevine was buzzing with the rumour that Georgy Knight was his latest conquest and if that was true then it wasn't surprising that he had lost interest, Phyllida thought wryly.

Yet she was sure that he had been waiting to intercept her that afternoon when she was sent with a message for Sister Charles on Mallory Ward. Ross had been standing by the stairs that were for staff use and out of bounds to patients and visitors and he watched her approach with an unmistakable gleam in his eyes.

Walking so quickly that he must have thought it an emergency at least, Phyllida had swept past him with the briefest of smiles and dashed up instead of down the stairs, knowing that he was about to descend. Then she had made her way to Mallory by a very roundabout route rather than risk running into him again.

To her chagrin, he had actually been with Sister

Charles in her office when she finally arrived to deliver a rather breathless message. Ross had raised an eyebrow at her flushed face and flyaway hair and for once there had been no hint of a smile in the dark eyes. Phyllida had felt very uncomfortable for he seemed to have a maddening ability for knowing just what was in her mind.

Now, she wondered if she had offended him. For it must have been very obvious that she didn't want to talk to him—and not because of an outmoded hospital ruling!

Well, she was off duty for a couple of days and she was rather thankful that she wouldn't see anything of him over the weekend. She needed that respite. For, try as she might to control it, her heart would leap just at the sound of his voice and did a crazy somersault whenever she saw him walk into the ward.

It was just an absurd physical attraction, of course. It would die a natural and inevitable death if she ignored it. She was a very long way from being in love with a man she scarcely knew. She didn't intend to entertain such a ridiculous idea for a moment!

But her hands lay idle in her lap, the tiny dress forgotten along with enchanting little Amy, the daughter of Phyllida's sister Drusilla who knew all about loving the wrong kind of man, and she drifted into a rather wonderful world inhabited by only two people. Herself and a very attractive and entirely reformed rake who declared that he wouldn't want any woman but her for the rest of his life.

It was an unlikely dream but delicious. Phyllida was level-headed enough to know that it would never come true and foolish enough, being all woman, to wish that it could . . .

On Saturday night, Phyllida put on her prettiest dress and her highest heels and brushed her newly-washed hair into a gleaming knot of curls for her date with Kevin Lawson.

She was rewarded by the instant admiration and approval in his eyes as she joined him in the communal sitting-room where nurses could entertain their men-friends as long as they left by midnight—and if one was sometimes sneaked into a nurse's flat or bed-sitting room when Sister Vernon's back was turned, then it was no other nurse's business to know about it!

Kevin had made several opportunities to talk to her on the ward during the last few days and the other nurses had begun to tease her about him. Phyllida didn't mind. She would rather they linked her name with Kevin's than suspect that she had a foolish weakness for Ross Harman. There was probably a degree of sexual intent in the houseman's interest in her, but Phyllida felt she could cope with it because she didn't find him at all attractive. She liked him as everyone did. But he was just another useful escort and likely friend, in her view.

Ross was something very different . . .

If she had known that Ross was a valuable member of the Hartlake rugger fifteen, she might have been pre-pared to see him at the dance. But she didn't and she wasn't and so her heart shook at the sight of him dancing with his arms about Georgy Knight.

Georgy was really very beautiful, Phyllida conceded fairly, although it hurt to realise that Ross obviously thought so, too. Fair and slender and so very sure of herself, she looked up at Ross, laughing—and he smiled into her eyes like a lover.

Phyllida looked away. She didn't think he had seen her. She didn't think he was particularly interested in whether or not she was present, anyway. She didn't think she ever wanted to see or speak to him again.

But she toyed with the rather comforting thought that he just might have asked her to come to this dance with him instead of Georgy if she hadn't so obviously avoided him for the last few days.

And knew it wasn't at all likely. For he'd probably asked Georgy long before he'd realised her existence. Phyllida reminded herself sensibly that she had been a very brief and unimportant interlude in a busy Casanova's life. She was sure that she'd been disappointing, too . . .

She danced with Kevin and allowed him to hold her close, to rest his cheek on her hair, to murmur all kinds of nonsense into her ear. For they both knew it *was* nonsense, amusing and harmless, meaning nothing. He didn't stir her senses and he certainly didn't quicken her heartbeat and there wasn't the least danger in being with him.

With an odd little ache somewhere in the region of her heart, Phyllida pretended that she was having a wonderful time. Kevin was easily deceived, being one of those people who couldn't imagine anyone not enjoying something as much as he did himself.

He was a very good dancer. He was admiring and attentive and she *ought* to be enjoying the evening. It was silly to hanker for a man who didn't want her and showed it!

Kevin went to the bar for drinks and became involved with some friends. Left alone at their table while the others in their group got up to dance, Phyllida watched the dancing couples, tapping a foot to the lively music quite unconsciously and waited for Kevin to come back.

She wouldn't admit even to herself that she was searching the softly-lit dance floor for a sign of Ross. She did see Georgy Knight, dancing with another man.

Someone put a hand on her shoulder. Phyllida turned, knowing that touch in the very depths of her being even before she looked into smiling dark eyes.

'Phyllida . . .'

She felt her heart catch at the way he said her name, turning it into an endearment. He couldn't mean it, of course. He just couldn't help making light love to every woman who crossed his path.

She smiled at him. 'Hallo, Ross.' The lack of surprise in eyes and voice was an unconscious betrayal that she had seen him that evening. She didn't realise how cool and uninterested she sounded, either.

'Enjoying yourself?'

'Very much,' she said brightly.

'What happened to Lawson?'

'Gone to get drinks.' She nodded towards the crowded bar.

'We've both been deserted,' he said lightly. 'Let's console each other. Come and dance with me!'

Phyllida glanced at Kevin, still talking. She doubted if he would mind if she danced with Ross. She thought it very likely that Georgy would! 'Why not?' she said, smiling, mentally cocking a snook at the staff nurse who was probably watching and fuming. Perhaps she would make her pay for it when she returned to the ward on Monday, but it would be worth it.

His arms felt so right as she slipped into them. He was just the right height for her, her head level with his broad shoulder. Their steps matched perfectly. Phyllida was glad that he didn't hold her too close for he might realise the thudding of her heart or sense the dawning desire in the secret depths of her body.

She didn't talk. She just drifted in his light embrace to the music and there wasn't anyone else in the world for her during those few moments, for all the crowd on the dance floor.

For the first time, Phyllida understood the intoxication that had swept her sister into a passionate affair with a married man with all its disastrous consequences.

She suddenly realised that it was very easy to resist temptation when one had never really been tempted. Now, she wanted Ross Harman with a swift, compelling urgency that was ready to throw all caution to the winds to find fulfilment in his arms.

She ached for the warmth of his lips and the kindling of passion in the way that he held her. She wanted him to want her as fiercely as she wanted him. She wanted the delight that he promised with his eyes, his touch, his nearness.

And she didn't dare to let him know it . . .

CHAPTER FOUR

Ross didn't know what he'd hoped, what he'd expected, when he impulsively made his way to her side. But the slight resistance that he sensed as they danced kept him from drawing her close as he wanted to do and her silence seemed to imply that she didn't want to talk to him. He wondered why she had agreed to dance with him if she didn't really like him.

She danced like a dream. Few girls could match their steps to his particular style of dancing with such ease. Phyllida moved in his arms as though they had danced together for years. She was not the kind of girl to take carelessly to bed with nothing but the mood of the moment in mind, he realised. She would probably need to believe herself in love before she went to bed with any man. Wanting her would get him nowhere unless he was prepared to commit himself to some extent. Ross wasn't too sure about that.

He liked her. She was sweet, very appealing, and she had character. But he wasn't ready to settle for one woman. He liked them all. He was a sensual man who had always taken whatever came his way in the past. There had been many casual, light-hearted and easily-forgotten conquests. Lots of Georgys, he thought wryly. Girls who gave their bodies and very little else and asked nothing of a man but a brief ecstasy. It was the way he had always wanted it.

She looked up at him with her swift and rather enchanting smile as the music stopped. Then his arms did tighten about her with a sudden reluctance to let her go. But a man didn't bring one girl to a dance and then desert her for another, whatever his inclination, he told himself firmly. And he had no reason to suppose that Phyllida would rather be with him than with the brash but popular Kevin Lawson.

There was some talk about the junior and the house-man, he knew. He didn't blame the man for taking an interest in Phyllida. He was slightly surprised that Lawson seemed to be her type, but one never knew anything about women, he had discovered. They lost their heads over the most unlikely men.

Her eyes widened, defensively. He smiled into them, reassuringly. 'You're a great little mover,' he said, light, teasing.

She laughed, eased herself out of his arms. 'I enjoyed it.'

'So did I. I'll be back for more,' he promised. He guided her through the crowd towards the still-empty table. 'Looks like you've lost your boy-friend.'

She resisted the impulse to point out that Kevin was nothing of the kind. 'He'll be back.'

'You're very sure of him.'

Phyllida shook her head, smiled. 'His car keys are in my bag.'

'Oh, I see. Very clever strategy,' he said, eyes dancing. 'You know a thing or two about men, obviously.'

' "Love me, love my car", in Kevin's case,' she agreed dryly. 'He's an enthusiast. I expect he's talking cars non-stop right now.'

'And I talked shop non-stop when I took you out.' His smile was very warm. 'Poor Phyllida. You must have been very bored.'

'No, I wasn't,' she said quickly. 'It was interesting. I liked listening to you.'

'Not enough to repeat the experience, I suspect.' His eyes twinkled at her. 'You've been avoiding me for days.'

The colour stormed into her face. She had hoped he hadn't noticed. She had certainly not expected him to embarrass her by mentioning it. 'I haven't!'

'You have, you know.'

She mustered a smile. 'Avoiding Sister's bad books, perhaps. She doesn't approve of nurses who talk to registrars!'

'And I don't approve of nurses who look through me,' he said quietly as she sat down at the table.

'I didn't! I smiled . . .' Too late, she knew that she had betrayed herself.

'Yes,' he said, wry. 'I *am* talking about yesterday. I'd rather you cut me dead than humour me with the kind of smile that you'd give a stranger. I thought we were friends.'

Phyllida wondered, rather surprised, if he had been more hurt than annoyed and knew how she would feel if he did the same to her.

'I'm sorry, Ross. I just didn't want to get involved,' she admitted with impulsive candour.

He looked down at her, thoughtful. 'Then? Or at all? I don't want to embarrass you. If you don't want to go out with me again, just say so now. I'll understand.'

She bit her lip. She didn't want to love him. She didn't

want to lose him, either, she thought in a sudden panic. '*I* don't understand what you want from me,' she said bluntly.

'But you suspect the worst?' He laughed and reached a hand to her cheek in the light caress that she already associated with him. 'Given half a chance, I'll make love to you, of course. That's fair warning, isn't it? But it isn't just your body that appeals to me. Trust me, Phyllida! I'm not such a heartless rake as you seem to think!'

She smiled. 'I expect you are! But I'll take a chance.'

'Good girl! You won't regret it,' he said, smiling with a warmth that hinted at enchantment.

'I'll take good care of that!' she said firmly.

About to leave her, he hesitated. 'These club dances get a bit out of hand as the evening wears on. Come and find me if Lawson doesn't take good care of you.'

It was nice of him to be concerned. But he was still going back to Georgy Knight, she thought, a trifle resentfully. She would have abandoned Kevin at a word if it had been spoken. Perhaps that proved that Ross was a much nicer person than herself, she thought dryly.

'Oh, I expect you'll have enough to do taking care of Georgy,' she said brightly.

'You *are* jealous,' he said, delighted.

He was gone before Phyllida could deny the amused accusation. Anyway, it was true, she admitted to herself. She didn't like his association with Georgy with all that it implied. She didn't like the self-satisfaction in the girl's expression as she passed by, dancing with Ross, only moments later. But he winked at Phyllida in a way that convinced her that he was only amusing himself with the staff nurse. Just like all the others.

Phyllida couldn't help wondering if he only wanted to sweep her into bed for all his assurances. What else could a man like Ross Harman want from a girl like herself, after all?

Her reluctance must seem an irresistible challenge to such a man. It was really the only likely explanation for his continued interest, she thought heavily. Why on earth did she allow him to charm her so easily?

'Sorry about that!' Kevin returned with the drinks at last. 'Got caught by the club bore and just couldn't get away,' he said cheerfully.

'That's all right. I had a dance with Ross Harman,' she said lightly.

'So I saw. Know him well, do you?'

'Not yet,' she said, a little mischievously.

He grinned. 'Aiming high, aren't you? Isn't a mere houseman good enough for you? I'm a damned sight safer!'

Phyllida sent him a sceptical smile. 'I doubt it!'

'I don't love 'em and leave 'em. Not too soon, anyway. People don't talk about me like they do about Harman.'

'Perhaps you're more discreet,' she suggested dryly.

Kevin laughed. 'Could be!' He held out a hand to her. 'Let's dance, darling . . .'

She rose and went into his arms, thinking that the endearment was very empty. It was odd but it seemed to her that Ross had spoken her name with more meaningful warmth than Kevin had conveyed with that too easily-used 'darling'.

Dancing with Kevin was an anti-climax. There was none of the magic and the enchantment she had found in Ross Harman's arms. There was no lift of her heart, no excitement in her veins. His lips were on her hair, straying towards her cheek, her mouth. She drew away slightly.

'Darling . . .' he said again, soft and slightly tense. 'Relax.'

'People are watching,' she said, lamely. *I don't do my kissing in public*, Ross had said. She admired him for that. She wished that Kevin would be a little more reticent. She wondered if she had been a little too encouraging. She didn't want Kevin to kiss her, in public or in private. Her heart caught at the thought of being kissed by Ross. She knew instinctively that it would be a magical experience.

Kevin's arms tightened. 'Do you care?'

'Yes. It's embarrassing,' she said with truth, feeling as though every eye was upon them.

He laughed. 'Okay. I'll save it for later,' he promised.

Later, she disliked the way he kissed her in his parked car outside the club-house, too sensually and too sure of her response. He had consumed a fair amount of alcohol and was inclined to be reckless as well as amorous.

Phyllida had gone into his arms to blot out the depressing vision of a very attractive Casanova making ardent love to a beautiful staff nurse. Now she was regretting it. She caught hold of a wandering hand. 'Do you mind!' she exclaimed, light but firm.

'Don't be a prude, sweetheart,' he chided. 'You're too pretty to act like a frigid old maid.' He drew her towards him. 'Besides, I've fallen in love with you!'

She didn't believe him and had no compunction in saying so. He was unrepentant. Phyllida supposed he had used that particular ploy to get what he wanted to good effect in the past, like so many men. Somehow she felt that Ross Harman was a cut above that kind of thing—or else women fell so readily into his arms he didn't need to resort to such strategies. Perhaps she was wrong but she couldn't help believing that when Ross told a girl that he loved her, it would be for real and for ever . . .

She sighed.

Kevin misinterpreted that soft little sound. He tried to kiss her again. She pushed him away.

'Don't spoil things!' he said impatiently.

It was ironic. Hadn't she said exactly the same thing to Ross, meaning something very different? It typified the difference in attitude of the sexes, she felt. A man was interested in sex for its own sake. A woman regarded sex as a very magical part of loving and felt cheapened when the two were separated.

She leaned forward to switch on the ignition. 'It's late. Time to go home,' she said decisively.

He groaned. 'You're a hard woman,' he reproached. 'No heart.' But he put the car into gear and steered it carefully out of the car park.

Phyllida was glad that it was only a short distance to Hartlake. She didn't think he was in any condition to drive. But at least he was not so drunk that he had been hard to handle, she thought thankfully. He was really a very nice person and she did like him. She didn't blame him for trying to make love to her just like any red-blooded male. She was used to fending off such advances. Only Ross had spent an evening with her and then left her without so much as a kiss. But he was so unpredictable that a woman might never know where she was with him!

She spent Sunday with her parents and sister and delightful small niece at her family home in Essex. It was near enough to visit on a day off but too far to travel back and forth to the hospital every day. Besides, she liked the freedom and the independence of living away from home and her parents had every faith in her level head. She wouldn't make the same mistake as the impulsive and rather wilful Drusilla, they felt.

Phyllida had been equally confident on that score until she went out with Ross and felt the rather alarming tug of his physical attractiveness. Now, she only hoped that she could continue to keep him at a safe distance. One kiss and she might melt into his arms, she thought ruefully, knowing what the mere touch of his hand could do to her.

She found a note in the letter rack addressed to her when she arrived back at the Nurses' Home late that night. It was from Ross, suggesting that they should spend the afternoon together as he happened to be free like herself.

Phyllida wondered what he had thought when she neither turned up at the suggested meeting place or let him know that she couldn't make it. She had left the Nurses' Home very early that morning, long before he could have left the brief but friendly note.

She was pleased and rather flattered that he had wanted her company. She might have been very torn between disappointing him and disappointing her family if she had known what was in his mind, she admitted.

She was in the ward kitchen renewing the patients' water jugs when he made an early visit to the ward. She caught just a glimpse of his tall figure and dark head as he passed the open door, white coat flying. It was impossible to go after him so she decided to try to catch him on his way from the ward.

He was behind drawn curtains with a patient and Georgy Knight when she went into the ward with the replenished water jugs. She could just hear the murmur of his deep, pleasant voice and the higher voice of the patient replying to his questions.

She set one of the jugs on a locker. The young girl in the bed caught at her arm. 'That's that nice Mr Harman,' she whispered, jerking her head at the closed curtains. 'Is he coming to examine me?'

She sounded so hopeful that Phyllida couldn't help smiling. But most women seemed to react to his looks and his charm. He had the perfect bedside manner, she thought dryly. He should make a very successful consultant.

'I'm not sure. Possibly.'

'You nurses are ever so lucky,' Julie Munro sighed enviously. 'All these good-looking doctors to work with. Wish *I* was a nurse!'

Phyllida tidied the variety of objects on top of the locker. 'Oh, we're less than the dust to doctors,' she said cheerfully. 'Just robots in uniform.'

'And we're just charts,' the girl said gloomily. 'He's only interested in my appendix. I don't think he ever looks at me face!' She giggled. 'He says I'll have a lovely scar, but I bet he'll never want to look at it once I'm out of here!'

Phyllida laughed. 'Just as well, isn't it? I don't think your boy-friend would be too pleased about it!'

'He's dead jealous. I can't even look at another bloke,' she said with satisfaction. 'Is your fella like that?'

'I haven't got one. No one special, anyway. Nurses don't have much time for romancing between work and study,' Phyllida said lightly.

The girl nudged her with a twinkle in her eye. 'Go on with you! I bet you find time to do a bit of romancing in the linen cupboard or the sluice with one of these young doctors!'

'You've been reading too many hospital romances.' She picked up the paperback lying on the locker and glanced at the title page. 'A doctor-nurse romance, I see. Good, is it?'

'Smashing. It's all about this handsome surgeon and a ward sister who fancies him but thinks he's practically engaged to a woman doctor and so she keeps snubbing him. Want to borrow it?'

'No, thanks.'

'Don't you like romance?'

'Not between the pages of a book.'

'Yeah. I know what you mean. All those happy endings. Lovely but not real, is it?'

'Oh, I don't know.' She tapped the girl's left hand with its neat diamond ring on the third finger. 'You're looking forward to your own happy ending, aren't you?'

'Good job this lot didn't happen on me honeymoon,' Julie giggled. 'I'll send you a bit of wedding cake, Nurse. Put it under your pillow and dream of the man you'll marry! I bet he'll wear a white coat!'

'For the wedding?' Phyllida chuckled. 'And we'll walk under an arch of crossed forceps, I suppose. Sounds original!'

'Nurse!' Georgy Knight looked round the drawn curtains of the next bed. 'A receiver—quickly!'

Phyllida hurried to get it. When she returned, she drew the curtain slightly to one side and entered the cubicle. The patient was looking very green but said that she no longer felt so sick.

'Well, Nurse will leave the bowl on the locker. Then if you are sick at all you won't need to panic,' Ross said reassuringly. 'Thank you, Nurse.'

He didn't look at Phyllida. She withdrew, dismissed. With Georgy Knight's suspicious eyes on them, she was glad he hadn't looked or smiled or given any hint that to him she wasn't just a robot in uniform as she had declared.

The curtains were drawn back and he moved on to Julie Munro, accompanied by the staff nurse. No examination this morning, apparently. Judging by the girl's expression of delight, he had told her that she could go home as everything was satisfactory and the wound was healing well.

Mrs Schwodler was going to Theatres that morning. The card above her bed warned staff that she was to have nil by mouth. She lay as stiff as a ramrod in the middle of the bed, petrified. She had reacted very badly to the anaesthetic after the first operation and this time she was convinced that she was going to die on the table.

Phyllida went to her side and reached for the tense fingers. 'Don't worry, Mrs Schwodler. You're going to be fine,' she said gently, soothing. 'It will soon be all over.'

'*Ach, nein* . . .' She sighed heavily.

'Mr Harman is just coming to talk to you and he'll explain it again.'

'*Ja?*' She struggled to sit up. 'I tell him *nein* . . . no operation. No more pain.'

'No more pain *after* the operation,' Phyllida said firmly. 'We've talked about it quite a lot and I expect you remember what I told you about my grandmother. I wish you could see her now . . . like a twenty year old!'

The old lady looked doubtful but seemed to be satisfied by Phyllida's confident manner. She didn't relax, but at least she didn't seem to be fighting the thought of surgery and before long she would be given the pre-med. Phyllida sent up a silent prayer that she would be all right. She wondered if Ross was operating. When he came so early to the ward it usually meant that he was due in Theatres.

As he approached the bed with Georgy Knight, she tried to catch his eye, to warn him with a meaningful glance that Mrs Schwodler was very apprehensive and needed reassurance. But he didn't seem to know that she existed that morning, his mind obviously on other things. She reminded herself that he was sensitive as well as very experienced and didn't need to be told what a patient was thinking and feeling. Good surgeons developed a very useful insight into the minds and hearts of their patients. She knew that Ross used it to good effect in his personal life, too.

She hovered in the corridor when she knew he was

about to leave the ward. But he came out with the staff nurse and Phyllida went into the clinical room and pretended to tidy the stock of surgical packs and enema packs and catheterisation packs.

She could hear their voices, his light and persuasive, Georgy's bright and laughing and obviously agreeing to something he was suggesting. Phyllida tried not to strain her ears and found herself hoping that he wasn't arranging yet another date with the girl.

She tiptoed to the open door and looked out just as they went into Sister's sitting-room and closed the door. To discuss the patients in privacy—or to snatch a few moments in each other's arms?

It was less than five minutes before he came out, alone. At last she had an opportunity to speak to him without Georgy Knight breathing down their necks!

His glance skimmed over her indifferently and then he strode off in the opposite direction. She hurried after him impulsively, wondering if he had even seen her standing by the swing doors of the ward. He had seemed so preoccupied . . .

'Mr Harman!'

He looked briefly over his shoulder without slackening pace. 'Sorry. No time,' he said brusquely.

Phyllida stopped short, feeling snubbed. He hadn't even softened the words with a glimmer of a smile.

No doubt he was due in Theatres, but he might have given her a few seconds to explain why she had apparently ignored his note. She was afraid that he might think she hadn't wanted to meet him. She was afraid that he was so annoyed at being stood up that he would never suggest another meeting. She was even more afraid that he was becoming much too important as her foolish heart sank almost to the floor at his curt and rebuffing attitude.

'Look out, Nurse—unless you want to come along for the ride!' The porter's cheerful warning made her step hastily to one side as the trolley with its drowsy patient was trundled towards the lift that would take her to the top floor where Theatres were situated.

Patients always spoke of 'going down' and the juniors soon gave up trying to correct them. Perhaps it had some connection with the thought of sinking into oblivion, Sister Tutor had suggested when one of the girls in Phyllida's set had queried the obstinacy of the patients in clinging to a false idea.

Phyllida glanced at the patient, but it wasn't Mrs Schwodler. Her operation was scheduled for ten-thirty and she wouldn't have her pre-med until about half an hour before she was taken to Theatres. Then she would receive another injection in the ante-room, given by the anaesthetist and jokingly called a Mickey Finn by the students because it acted so quickly.

She went back to the ward and got on with the routine chores and tried not to think about Ross. He might not have meant to humiliate her but she didn't mean to invite another snub.

In future, she would remember that it just wasn't etiquette for a junior nurse to approach a senior registrar, on or off the wards!

CHAPTER FIVE

KEVIN came into the sluice and sneaked an arm about Phyllida's waist. 'How's my angel?'

She was up to her elbows in hot water, face flushed and soft bright curls escaping from the knot at the back of her head. She put a wet hand to a flyaway strand of hair and pushed it off her face.

'I'm nobody's angel,' she said wearily. 'I'm hot and tired and my feet ache and I can't think why I wanted to nurse!'

'Dedication?' he suggested, grinning. 'Job satisfaction?'

She sent him a sceptical glance. 'Not much job satisfaction in washing out bedpans! Georgy Knight's had me running round in circles today. She's thrown all the unpleasant jobs in my direction.' She knew why, too, she thought wryly. Georgy had certainly seen her dancing with Ross on Saturday night and she was being punished for encouraging him.

'Never mind, love. I'll make it up to you tonight,' Kevin promised.

'Tonight?'

'Come round to the flat and put your aching feet up and be spoiled,' he said persuasively. 'I'll even feed you into the bargain.'

Phyllida hesitated. 'I don't know. I really ought to study . . .'

'Bring your books with you and study in comfort,' he said promptly. 'And if you need any help with Anatomy just say the word. It's my best subject!' There was meaningful mischief behind the words.

Nice as he was and much as she liked him, she wasn't tempted. She trusted him and so she had no qualms about spending an evening alone in his flat with him. She was very sure that she could handle a situation if one should develop, anyway. He might be an opportunist like most men but she had already found that he could take no for an answer. But she didn't feel like going out that evening. She didn't feel much like studying, either, she admitted ruefully. And if it had been Ross Harman instead of Kevin issuing the invitation, she probably wouldn't have hesitated—and she didn't trust *him* at all!

'Honestly, Kevin, I don't think I'd be very good company this evening,' she said truthfully.

He looked at her thoughtfully. 'I know I was rather sloshed on Saturday. The latter part of the evening is somewhat hazy. Did I say or do something totally unforgivable?'

She smiled, shook her head. 'No, of course not!'

'It doesn't sound like me,' he said in mock surprise. 'I must have been more drunk than I knew!'

She laughed, warming to him. 'Idiot!'

He moved closer and dropped a light kiss on the back of her neck. 'Did I tell you that I love you? I do, you know.'

She wriggled away from him, undisturbed and unimpressed. 'You probably say that to all your girlfriends!'

'And it works,' he assured her lightly, quite unrepentant, a twinkle in his eyes.

He talked like a rake. Phyllida didn't think he was a very successful womaniser, in fact. He was too nice, too gentle and considerate and kind. She felt that a man had to be very selfish and heartless to take his sexual satisfaction with a succession of women who didn't mean very much to him—and that was *her* definition of a rake.

'Dó come,' Kevin urged. 'I'm a great cook.'

'The way to a hard-working nurse's heart,' she conceded, smiling. 'All right. I'll come. Now you'd better scoot before Georgy catches us talking. I'm not one of her favourite people, you know.'

It was too late. Even as she spoke, the staff nurse appeared in the doorway. 'It is you, Dr Lawson! I thought I recognised the voice. I was just about to "bleep" for you. Mrs Barnes is running a slight fever and is being persistently sick. Would you have a look at her?'

'Certainly. She did warn me that she reacts badly to anaesthetic and she was in Theatres for rather a long time,' he said easily. 'I'll prescribe something to stop the sickness . . . '

Before the staff nurse followed him, she looked at Phyllida with dislike. 'You needn't make quite so much clatter with those bedpans. I'm not impressed. It was suspiciously quiet in here just now. If you didn't spend so much time flirting with anything in a white coat you'd have more time for your work!'

'Yes, Staff,' she said meekly.

Georgy disappeared with an indignant whisk of her starched skirts. Phyllida heaved a sigh. It seemed that nothing she did was right. Georgy ought to be pleased that she was encouraging the houseman instead of Ross Harman! If she followed her heart rather than her head, she would be doing all she could to attract the registrar, after all!

Later in the afternoon, sent to make up a bed for a new admission, Phyllida went to the linen cupboard for sheets. As she emerged, arms full, she collided with Ross as he hurried along the corridor.

'Sorry!'

'You ought to wear a bell round your neck, nurse,' he said without humour.

Phyllida flushed. 'You weren't looking either!' she said sharply and with spirit.

'I'm in a hurry.' His tone was curt.

'So am I! Georgy Knight thinks I've three pairs of hands and I wish I had! She's making my life a misery, thanks to you!' she told him impulsively.

Up went that eyebrow in familiar, slightly mocking fashion at the retort which dismissed any claim he might have to the respect of a very junior nurse for his position and authority. 'Could it be your tendency to cause havoc at every turn rather than anything I've said or done?' he suggested.

She flashed him an indignant look. 'You know very well that she's furious because you danced with me on Saturday night. She sees you as her property!'

'I don't belong to any woman.' He spoke quickly, very firm. 'And I've yet to meet one who doesn't think she owns me on the strength of one date!' The rider was cutting.

Perhaps she was over-sensitive but Phyllida instantly bridled. 'There's *me*!' she declared tartly. 'I don't feel like that about you!'

He regarded her thoughtfully. 'No, I don't think you

do,' he agreed, slightly amused. 'You have another distinction, too. You're the first girl to stand me up!'

'I tried to explain about that,' she said proudly. 'You didn't have time to listen.'

'And I haven't time now,' he said with the rueful smile that charmed and disarmed most women. He put a hand on her arm, very briefly. 'Meet me tonight and we'll sort it out. Same time and place as before?'

He was already moving away from her for he was answering an urgent summons from the Intensive Care Unit and he had lost valuable time in pausing to talk to her.

'I can't make it tonight!'

He didn't pause to differentiate between regret and indifference. His eyes narrowed abruptly. 'Can't—or won't?' he demanded brusquely.

'I've another date . . .' She began to explain.

He cut her short. 'Fair enough!' She wasn't just playing hard to get, he thought, disappointed. She just wasn't interested and he might as well accept the fact. But it was hard for a man who had always reached out and taken any woman he wanted with smiling ease.

He was gone and there was something in the set of the broad shoulders and the tilt of the dark head that told Phyllida of unspoken anger. He didn't believe her, of course. He thought it was just another brush-off.

And in a way, it was. For it would have been a simple matter to consign her date with Kevin to the limbo of another day. She could have invented an excuse he would accept so that she was free to meet Ross that evening.

Perhaps her level head was dictating her responses and perhaps it was just as well, she thought wryly. For all her emotions seemed bound up in wanting Ross too much for her own good!

She sighed and went back to the ward and was scolded by Georgy Knight for taking so long to collect a couple of sheets. The staff nurse was obviously suspicious and Phyllida wondered if she thought that she'd lured Ross into the linen cupboard for a kiss and a cuddle. No such luck!

Making up the bed for the new admission, she hoped that he hadn't felt snubbed. It was the last thing she wanted. For it was flattering that he was being so persistent even if caution and common sense warned her that it was not the kind of pursuit she should welcome or encourage.

Somehow, she must make an opportunity to show him that she wasn't as indifferent as the circumstances might indicate. It was just unfortunate that she hadn't known about his note until it was too late to do anything about it—and even more unfortunate that she'd relented and accepted Kevin's invitation before she knew that Ross wanted to see her that evening.

Phyllida was thankful when it was time to go off duty that evening. Before leaving the ward, she looked in on Mrs Schwodler who was being specialled in a side ward. She was heavily sedated. Helen Buckley sat by the bed watching the machines that monitored the patient's heartbeat and respirations, checking the steady flow of intravenous drips and aspirating the nasal tube, alert for any emergency.

'How is she?' Phyllida asked softly.

'Not too well just now.'

'Will she do?'

Helen had seen death too many times not to know that its shadow was hovering. But she didn't say so for she knew that Phyllida was very concerned.

'Mr Harman seems very confident that she'll pull through,' she said reassuringly.

She saw that Phyllida's expression brightened immediately and she wondered if it was the cheerful prognosis or the mention of Ross Harman's name.

Helen was an observant and sensitive girl and she saw more than Phyllida knew. She had no intention of saying anything or offering probably unwelcome advice, but she was a little sorry that the first-year's fancy had alighted on a heartless rake. She had been just as impressed by his attractions and as flattered by his attentions when he took a brief interest in her and although her heart hadn't been broken when he moved on to someone else, it had felt rather bruised for some time. He was such an attractive devil and he knew just how to charm a girl into giving him what he wanted. Georgy Knight was the latest of his conquests and proud of it. Helen suspected that Phyllida would be the next and that seemed a pity. For she was a very nice girl who deserved better than heartache and humiliation at Ross Harman's hands.

Helen wondered if she could trade on their past relationship and try to persuade him not to take advantage of a girl who had too much heart and not enough experience of men like him and decided, knowing Ross, to say nothing. For he would probably delight in laying siege to Phyllida if he thought that it annoyed a past love, she thought shrewdly. She had no illusions about Ross . . .

Kevin's flat was little more than a bed-sitter in one of the tall, terraced houses in Clifton Street and it was neither comfortable nor cheerful. Phyllida settled herself on the lumpy sofa with the books that she didn't expect to open while he pottered about between the tiny electric cooker and the ancient sink. She didn't know what he was preparing for their supper but the smell was appetising, bearing out his claim to be a good cook.

'Surely you don't sleep on this!' she exclaimed, shifting her position to avoid a particularly hard lump in the cushions.

He glanced over his shoulder, grinned. 'Do I seem like a masochist? There's a pull-down bed inside that cupboard affair. Which means that I never have to make it as it's always shoved out of sight.'

She wrinkled her nose. 'Charming!'

He moved towards the sofa. 'I know it's pretty sordid, but it suits my pocket and my purpose for the time being. I won't be a houseman for ever. I shall be a Harley Street man with a lucrative private practice and a big house in Hampstead within a few years. Wait and see!'

'I don't doubt it,' she said lightly.

'So this place serves while I'm walking the wards.'

'It wouldn't be so bad if you brightened it up with some paint and fresh paper,' Phyllida pointed out with the cheerful frankness that was only possible between friends.

'I'm a doctor, love. Not a decorator!' he told her blithely. 'Anyway, you brighten the place with that pretty face.' He bent to drop a kiss on her curls. 'I'm glad you came tonight, Phyllida. We haven't had much chance to be on our own and really get to know each other.'

She smiled. 'Don't pin your hopes on knowing me too well,' she warned. 'That bed stays out of sight while I'm here—and this sofa's so lumpy that I doubt if any girl could be tempted to give her all on it!'

He laughed, delighted. 'You won't notice the lumps once I get my arms round you,' he promised.

'You'll notice a few lumps if you don't behave yourself,' she assured him light-heartedly, brandishing a heavy textbook.

He caught her wrist and ran his thumb over the velvety inner flesh of her arm. 'I won't do anything you don't want me to do, darling,' he said softly, eyes dancing.

'That's a double-edged assurance—and I've heard it before. I'm not as green as you seem to think,' she told him firmly.

'You're very lovely.'

She was slightly disturbed by the meaningful tone. 'How's my supper?' she demanded to lighten the sudden tension. 'I hope you didn't get me here on false pretences!'

Instantly, he followed her lead. 'One taste of my goulash and you'll fall into my arms,' he said confidently. 'It's irresistible . . . '

It was certainly good. Phyllida enjoyed the food and the wine he served with it. After the meal, she helped him to clear away and wash up. They put on some records and chatted over coffee and then watched a variety show on his small television set. Later, she listened while he talked about himself, his family and his reasons for becoming a doctor. She knew some of it, but she didn't mind hearing it again.

She felt that he lacked the initiative and drive of a Ross Harman and would probably settle for general practice. He wasn't ambitious, despite the light-hearted talk of a Harley Street practice. He just wanted to be a reasonably good doctor in a quiet country town, like his father before him.

He was a pleasant and reliable young man who would make some girl a good husband in due course. Just now, he wasn't even thinking about marriage. But that didn't stop him from falling in love—frequently! Hartlake provided lots of opportunities for light-hearted romance, after all.

When he put an arm about Phyllida and drew her close, she didn't resist. When he kissed her, she didn't protest. His kiss was very nice and totally unexciting. She wondered why her senses didn't stir in the slightest at his kiss or his touch or his obvious longing . . . and leaped to instant, throbbing life for one glance from Ross Harman's dark and glowing eyes.

He kissed her again. 'Darling,' he sighed against her lips. 'I do love you . . . ' His lips strayed to her throat, the long line of her neck and just hinted at the route to her breast.

Phyllida stroked the fine blond hair—and found herself thinking of crisp, dark curls that promised to cling to her fingers if she should dare to touch them.

She was a little anxious about the throb of unexpected sincerity in Kevin's voice. She didn't want him to love her. She didn't believe that he did. But he might be on the threshold of loving and she didn't want to hurt and disappoint him.

She thought wryly that it seemed so easy for him to talk of loving while another man had probably never said it to any woman in his life. Somehow she knew instinctively that it would mean very much more if Ross ever told a woman that he loved her. Phyllida sensed that he was capable of great depth of feeling, yet to be stirred to life. He would not speak the words lightly and, once spoken, he would never regret or retract them, she felt. If he ever loved, it would be for always and be the kind of loving that enriched a woman's life with real and lasting happiness.

She felt a little pang of envy of that unknown woman in his future. She realised that she was not the woman he was destined to love. She was too immature and too inexperienced and too ordinary for a man like Ross. Well, she didn't mean to lose her heart to him. But she wondered if the feelings he inspired would ever be awakened and fulfilled by any other man.

Having known the kindling of that flame, she knew she couldn't feel anything for Kevin but a mild affection and it wasn't fair to encourage him to care for her. So she must cool the relationship here and now as she had done with other men in the past.

'Don't get too serious, Kevin,' she said quietly, very gently.

'Too late, love,' he said, smiling into her eyes.

She drew away from him slightly, troubled. 'You'll only get hurt,' she warned.

'I'll take that chance.' He traced the lovely line of her cheek until his lips reached the corner of her mouth.

Then he kissed her and this time his lips lingered with a little passion. 'You aren't like other girls,' he murmured, meaning it. 'I can't help loving you . . . '

'You mustn't love me,' she told him firmly. 'We're just friends.'

His arms tightened about her. 'Can't friends be lovers, too?' he asked, warm, persuasive. 'Relax, darling. Kiss me . . . '

She kissed him reluctantly, very light. As his embrace became more ardent, she pushed him away with both hands against his chest. 'It's time I went home.'

'Not yet! It's only eleven o'clock!' he protested swiftly.

'I know. But it's been a long day.' She smiled at him. 'It's been fun this evening and I've enjoyed it. We can do it again if you'll accept that friends don't have to be lovers. I'm sorry if I gave you the wrong impression, but I'm not the kind of girl who sleeps around.'

'I know you're not! That's what I said! You're different—and that's what I love about you, Phyllida.'

She wondered dryly how long he would continue to love her if she insisted on keeping him at arms' length. Rising, she began to gather up her neglected books. He helped her, brought her coat and held it while she slipped her arms into it. She liked the way he swallowed disappointment and showed no sign of resentment. He was really a very nice person. It was almost a pity that she didn't feel that she could ever love him . . .

As they left the house, hand in hand and laughing together at some absurdity, a car drew up and parked a little way down the narrow street.

'Ross Harman,' Kevin said carelessly, glancing at the easily recognisable car.

Phyllida's heart lurched. 'Does he live there?'

'Lord no! Registrars can afford better than Clifton Street,' he said without envy. 'He's just bringing Georgy Knight home. It's getting to be a regular thing. Didn't you know?'

To bear out his words, Ross held out his hand to Georgy to help her from the car as they drew level. He glanced at Kevin and Phyllida, nodded in reply to the houseman's friendly greeting. Phyllida, meeting Georgy's triumphant eyes, read the unmistakable message in their depths and wondered how she had betrayed herself. For Georgy certainly knew how she felt about Ross and was delighting in his preference for her. She only hoped that Ross didn't know it, too!

He had quickly found a substitute companion for the evening. She couldn't blame him for that, of course . . . and it would be unreasonable to expect him to care one way or the other that she had not been free to meet him. Any more than he cared that her date had been with Kevin. His eyes skated over her face with indifference and his smile was cursory. Anyone would think he had never seen her before or didn't recognise her out of uniform!

Then Georgy tucked her hand possessively into his arm and drew him towards the house and Phyllida walked on with Kevin, trying not to feel that she hated the beautiful and much too confident staff nurse, trying not to think that they would soon be locked in each other's arms.

He was a heartless rake. Georgy was a light-hearted

flirt who flitted from man to man. They suited each other. Like to like . . . and what did she have in common with Ross Harman that she felt so drawn to him and longed so much for them to be friends—and maybe even more than friends, she thought recklessly. For why should she cling so desperately to her virginity when it seemed that almost every other girl set out to lose it as soon as possible and won the most attractive men as a result?

Kevin had called her a prude. Ross treated her like a schoolgirl. She was beginning to feel like a freak. She had sometimes felt that girls of her particular generation were brainwashed into permissive sexuality and at last she understood how and why it happened.

But she still didn't mean to go to bed with a man just because he wanted her, she told herself firmly. And thought wryly that it was just as well that Ross was much too busy with the Georgy Knights of this world to want her. For she might not be able to resist the temptation in his brand of charm . . .

CHAPTER SIX

MRS SCHWODLER'S condition worsened during the night and her name was entered on the seriously-ill list when Phyllida came on to the ward for the day's work. Ross was already there. He was in the side ward with the curtains drawn across the observation window, assisted by Sister as they worked on the old lady. Phyllida learned later that he had carried out an emergency tracheotomy.

Busy with the ward routine, her thoughts were with Mrs Schwodler who had slipped into the coma that usually preceded death. Ross was in and out of the ward throughout the day, keeping a watchful eye on his patient.

Phyllida didn't expect him to have time for a very unimportant first-year nurse in the middle of a crisis. He looked through her when she passed him at the ward desk, talking to Sister and Georgy Knight. He nodded, unsmiling and remote, when she murmured a hasty apology for trundling a trolley across his path as he emerged from the side ward. He looked so anxious that she forgave him.

She admired the man whose caring concern for one sick old lady must surely outweigh his uncaring attitude to the women in his personal life. After all, he probably had his priorities right. His patients were more important than his women, a matter of life or death compared with the trivialities of a bruised heart or a wounded pride.

Phyllida was anxious, too. Despite Sister Tutor's advice, she had developed an affection for Mrs Schwodler and she had so wanted her to come through surgery without complications and get well. She didn't want her to die when she had virtually promised that her life was safe in the clever and capable hands of Ross Harman.

She slipped into the side ward when an opportunity offered. Mrs Schwodler was a cyanosed stranger among a mass of tubes and sophisticated equipment and Phyllida's eyes widened. Sister looked round with a slight frown.

'I'm sorry, Sister . . .' Phyllida hadn't known that she was briefly relieving a nurse in the duty of 'specialling' the patient.

'What is it, Nurse Sims?'

'Nothing . . . I mean—I just wanted . . .' She trailed off, biting her lip. She suddenly knew that there was no real hope for Mrs Schwodler. 'I liked her,' she said simply.

Sister Hamilton softened and put a hand on her arm. 'Yes, I know. She was a gentle soul. Sit with her for a few minutes while I speak to her daughter, Nurse. You won't need to do anything for her. Just watch the monitor for any signs of failing.'

'Yes, Sister.'

Phyllida sat down and glued her eyes to the monitor that recorded the heartbeat. The trace was weak and faltering and, left alone, she was convinced that at any moment it would simply peter out and the sudden shrill tone that signified heart failure would tell its own story.

The old lady was in deep coma, but Phyllida reached for the thin hand and clasped it as though her own vital life force could impart some of itself into the failing spirit. She sat, tense and rigid, willing Mrs Schwodler to rally and pull through against all expectations.

Someone came in. Thinking it was Sister, Phyllida rose, half-turned. It was Ross.

'Sit down, Nurse. I'm only checking if there's any change,' he said quietly, formally. He felt for the pulse, raised an eyelid and shone his pencil torch into the pupil, followed the trace on the monitor with a faint frown. 'She's failing . . . '

'How long?' Phyllida asked impulsively.

'I've no idea. Minutes, hours. We could put her on life-support and keep heart and lungs functioning indefinitely, but she's an old lady and I don't think it will serve any purpose. There may be some brain damage already, anyway.'

'All these tubes . . . ' She gestured towards the bed. 'Are they really necessary now?'

'She'll die very quickly without them,' he said bluntly.

'She'll die with dignity!'

He raised an eyebrow. 'It's an emotive point of view. It's my job to do everything I can for as long as I can. As a nurse, you should know that.'

'But not *"strive officiously to keep alive"*,' she said quickly.

'No. Which explains why she isn't on life support,' he said coolly.

Phyllida felt reproved. She was silent.

Ross looked at her thoughtfully, aware that she was

upset and wondering if it was her first such experience. She was a very junior nurse, after all.

'Ever coped with a patient's death?' he asked abruptly. She shook her head. 'It's as natural as birth and without the trauma in this kind of case,' he assured her. 'Just a sigh between this life and the next. Some juniors are nervous, even frightened. There's no need, believe me.'

She wasn't frightened. Just saddened. But it was nice of him to reassure her. He went before she could say so, thank him. But she would remember his consideration for her inexperience.

Very soon, Sister returned to relieve her and send her back to the ward. As Phyllida turned to go with a murmur of thanks, the monitor sounded its sharp note of finality and she swung back, an exclamation of dismay flying to her lips.

Sister Hamilton moved swiftly to the bedside, began to disconnect tubes and equipment so that the daughter would not be too distressed by her mother's condition. 'Very well, Nurse Sims . . . off you go! There's nothing more for you to do here,' she said, deliberately brisk because she saw the quiver of that sensitive mouth.

Ross, no longer looking anxious but relaxed and smiling, was talking to Georgy Knight by the ward desk. She was smiling back at him with a hint of remembered intimacy in her beautiful eyes. The rapport between them was quite unmistakable and had nothing to do with their respective roles as surgeon and staff nurse, Phyllida knew.

She rushed from the ward, eyes flooding with tears,

quite unable to approach either of them or anyone else until she had mastered her emotions.

She hurried blindly along the corridor to the spacious linen cupboard, sanctuary of tearful nurses since the days of Florence Nightingale. Fortunately, it was empty. There, in the dark little room, she rested her head against a stack of towels and sobbed out her heart for more than the death of a gentle old lady.

She didn't really know what she mourned but Mrs Schwodler's death was all mixed up with the very casual attitude of a man who seemed to prefer the obvious and striking attractions of a staff nurse to anything that she could offer.

Someone came in and switched on the light and drew her into strong, comforting arms. Phyllida buried her face against his broad shoulder, although the tears were instantly checked by the almost painful leap of her heart. She didn't need to look up and into his handsome face to know that it was Ross. Her body would remember his touch until her dying day.

It was an entirely sexless and almost impersonal embrace. She didn't know how rigidly he controlled his emotions as he held her. She only knew that he soothed and talked to her as though she was a child, patting her shoulder and stroking the soft, capless curls and murmuring the absurd little comforts that gradually quietened the tumult of her heart and mind.

'Feeling better?' he asked at last, his arms relaxing their hold.

Phyllida drew away from him, convinced that he was just being kind. It was an unexpected glimpse of a side to him that she hadn't known, catching at her heart. At the same time, it was dismaying that he could be so unmoved by her nearness.

'Yes. Thanks . . .' She didn't sound grateful, she knew. It wasn't easy to feel grateful. Kindness was cold comfort when a woman wanted a man who just didn't want her in the same way!

'I thought I'd find you in here,' he said, smiling at her with warm understanding. 'You aren't the first nurse to need a bolt-hole on occasions—and you won't be the last.'

She smiled shakily. 'I feel an awful idiot,' she said with truth.

'Nonsense! You needed a good cry, that's all. Now you can put it behind you.' He hesitated. 'Can I give you some good advice?' he went on gently. 'Do try not to get too attached to people, Phyllida. You'll only get hurt in the long run.'

He might have been referring to patients. She felt that he was warning her against liking him too much. Her heart welled with a tide of humiliation. Was she so obvious? Had she gone too readily into those comforting arms? Had he sensed the need of him that went so much deeper than distress over the death of a patient?

Or had Georgy Knight been spilling a little venom, she wondered shrewdly. The staff nurse certainly suspected her weakness for Ross and she wasn't beyond hinting at it with assumed indulgence.

He was the kind of man who would instantly back away if he thought a girl was beginning to care for him, Phyllida thought wryly. It might demand too much of him. It might complicate his pleasant and utterly selfish way of life. Well, he had nothing to fear from her, she determined proudly.

'I'll remember,' she said carefully. 'Thanks again . . . '

'My pleasure,' he drawled and his dark eyes smiled. 'Call on me any time you feel like a good cry. I'll always oblige with a convenient shoulder. It's what friends are for.'

She smiled uncertainly. Friends but never lovers. He was making it very clear. Just as she had for Kevin. But as she met his eyes and felt that odd little flutter of her heart and the alarming stir of her senses, she knew that she wanted him for a lover and that friendship could look after itself!

But she didn't dare to say so or even to hint at it with eyes or smile or attitude.

She took refuge in the mundane. 'I'd better get back to the ward . . . '

He stooped to pick up the rebellious cap that seemed to spend more time on the floor than adorning her bright curls.

'Wash that pretty face before you do,' he suggested lightly. 'Or everyone will know that you've been shedding tears—and I might get the blame!'

'Oh no! Why should you? Everyone knows that you don't take much interest in first-years,' she said, a little brightly.

'That doesn't seem to stop the first-years from taking an interest in me,' he said dryly. 'Except you, of course. Sometimes I feel that you don't even like me, Phyllida.'

She felt a betraying warmth steal into her face. 'Why shouldn't I like you?' she said as lightly as she could. 'You've never done me any harm.' She tried to pin on her cap without the aid of a mirror so that she had something to do with her hands. For she was terribly tempted to reach out to him, to prove just how much she did like him. She ached to put her arms about him and kiss him. She knew it was a desperate need for reassurance. No woman liked to think that she was so unattractive in the eyes of a very sensual man, after all.

Ross leaned against a shelf, arms folded across his chest, a little smile lurking in the depths of his eyes as he watched her fumbling attempts with the ridiculous triangle of starched linen.

'You don't give me much opportunity,' he said. He made light of it, but he found it disconcerting and dismaying that she kept him so firmly at a distance.

She turned a laughing face to him. 'I've heard too much about you!'

'You can trust me. I wouldn't harm a hair of your head,' he said warmly. 'I like you too much.' He wondered why he didn't just catch her close and kiss the soft sweet mouth that was so much temptation. Such tactics had always been very successful in the past. But he was sure that they wouldn't be welcomed by Phyllida.

Her heart somersaulted. But he only spoke of liking, she cautioned herself sternly. Damned with faint praise! Perhaps she should be gratified but it was a terrific let-down. Liking—from a man like Ross Harman!

She reached to brush his lean cheek with her lips, so lightly that it wasn't a kiss at all. 'You're really much nicer than you want anyone to know, Ross Harman,' she told him, so lightly that she left him wondering if she meant the words at all. Then she turned to the door and opened it cautiously, half-expecting to find Georgy

Knight waiting for them to emerge from the cupboard. She glanced along the deserted corridor with relief. 'All clear!' she exclaimed thankfully and hurried towards the juniors' room to make herself tidy before presenting herself to Sister with an apology and an explanation for her absence.

Ross looked after the trim figure and thought wryly that he would have to accept that this was one girl he wasn't going to win. He knew enough about women to recognise when one didn't want him—and Phyllida simply wasn't interested.

He couldn't blame her. She was probably wise to steer clear of tangling with a man like himself. She was safer in the arms of someone like Kevin Lawson. For he didn't think he could trust himself to respect the enchanting innocence and obvious inexperience despite his promise.

He wanted her too much.

Too much to accept defeat without one more try . . .

Phyllida crossed Main Hall on her way from the ward at the end of the day's work, tired, rather dispirited and thinking of a hot bath, a lazy evening and an early night. Kevin had asked her to go to the pictures with him but she had persuaded him to make it another night. She just didn't feel like going out that evening.

She saw Ross by the big reception desk, talking to Jimmy, the Head Porter. She was surprised that he was still around, remembering that he had been on Paterson when she arrived that morning. He had worked a very long day.

He saw her and smiled . . . the slow, warm and very

enchanting smile that ought not to melt her heart but did. She could not help smiling back at him with encouraging warmth. With a word to Jimmy, he began to walk towards her and Phyllida was very conscious of the big man's interested gaze.

Jimmy was an institution at Hartlake and the main source of the hospital grapevine and he had a gift for scenting romance—often where none existed! She didn't want her name linked with Ross Harman as it inevitably would be if they were seen too obviously in each other's company!

'I hoped to see you,' he said lightly and fell into step with her as she continued towards the main doors. She didn't want to stand talking to him in Main Hall, focus of attention. 'Feeling happier?'

She smiled ruefully. 'Yes, of course. You were very kind. I didn't thank you.'

He seized the opportunity. 'You can thank me by having a drink with me. We'll forget all about Hartlake and talk about ourselves for an hour.'

'Oh, Ross, I've so much to do this evening,' she said, a little lamely, so tempted that she felt it must be wiser to say no.

His eyes narrowed. 'Doing it with Lawson?'

She was startled by the brusque demand into a hasty denial. 'No . . .'

'Then you can spare me an hour,' he said, very firm. 'I won't take you to the Kingfisher this time. We'll go where no one knows us. My car's outside.' He drew her through the swing doors, guiding her through the stream of people making their way into the hospital to visit friends and relatives.

'Like this?' she demurred.

'Just as you are—and very charming you look, too,' he told her, smiling.

His smile was magic. So was the touch of his hand on her arm. Phyllida felt he was a weakness that she ought to resist. 'I'm really rather tired . . .'

'Phyllida!' It was a reproach, gentle but unmistakable.

Meeting the dark, slightly amused eyes, she felt foolish. Of course, he was just being friendly and she had no reason to be on the defensive. She should be pleased that he wanted to be with her and obviously had no intention of whisking her into bed at the first opportunity. He liked her and looked on her as a friend and that was flattering. She didn't want him to regard her as a sexual object like all the other women he had known. It was a relief that he didn't. She had no need to be on her guard. He was entirely to be trusted, she felt. She wished she could trust the way she felt about him, she thought wryly. He needed protecting from her! She might be too tempted to make love to him!

'Half an hour, then,' she conceded, so careful not to sound too eager for his company that it came out cool.

Immediately, he stiffened, frowned. 'Don't do me any favours!' he said, angry. 'I thought we had something to give each other. It seems I was wrong!'

She caught at his arm as he turned away. 'I didn't mean to be ungracious,' she said quickly. 'It's been a rotten day and I just don't feel like being sociable.'

'Then we'll leave it for another time,' he told her, curt.

Her heart sank. She had really offended him—again! She wondered why their friendship was so uncertain and unpredictable when it ought to run so smoothly. For they liked each other. They didn't ask or expect very much from each other. So what kept going wrong? Something certainly did.

She was too proud to show disappointment, to plead for a second chance. 'Yes, I think so,' she agreed, trying so hard to be light-hearted that she sounded indifferent. 'You do understand, don't you?'

'Perfectly. Goodnight, Phyllida.' He strode away, unsmiling.

She stood uncertain on the pavement, wanting to run after him and knowing that it was impossible. He *didn't* understand, she thought heavily, turning to walk towards the Nurses' Home and the bleakness of an evening that would have been very different if she hadn't been so clumsy in her handling of his invitation.

He thought she snubbed him because she didn't want to be too involved with him although he was only offering a very ordinary friendship. Phyllida knew that she wanted much more than his liking and a mild affection. She wanted him to love her as she was beginning to love him—and that was too much to ask of a man like Ross. Besides, the first step towards loving had to be a sexual attraction. For all his opportunities, he had never once attempted to kiss her!

She had to face facts. He was just taking a kindly interest in a girl that he had probably only noticed in the first place because of her reputation for clumsiness. And was she living up to it! On and off the ward! No wonder he was becoming impatient with her. Soon he would give up and stop asking her out and dismiss her completely.

It was the best thing that could happen, she told herself firmly. She was too near to loving him and there

was no future in that! And there was too much risk of
showing it and that would embarrass them both and ruin
their relationship, anyway.

She tried to shake off a slight depression as she
reached the flat in the Nurses' Home that she shared
with her three friends. She didn't want them noticing
and wondering and perhaps putting two and two
together.

Kate was too caught up in her own affair with one of
the housemen to take much notice of anything else.
Jacqui was a quiet girl who seemed intent on making
Nurse of the Year and seldom left her books to enjoy
herself with any of the men who sought her out, not
seeming to realise that she was pretty and popular. But
Patti was particularly perceptive, rather older than most
of their set and more experienced in the kind of heartache that a man could cause and she took a protective
interest in their affairs.

The girls had known about that first date in the
Kingfisher with Ross, of course. They had teased her,
but Phyllida had only laughed and assured them it had
been a very casual meeting. Since then, in self-defence,
she had tended to make more of her meetings with Kevin
Lawson than they deserved and avoided any mention of
the registrar.

They didn't know about her encounters with him on
the ward—and none of them were worth recounting or
remembering, after all. Even that afternoon, taking all
kinds of risks by being in the linen cupboard with him
and not the least of them being instant dismissal, he had
embraced her like a brother or an uncle. She doubted if
it would have made a scrap of difference if he'd known

that she wasn't feeling in the least like his sister or niece as she stood in his arms, heart pounding and desire crashing in tumultuous waves through her trembling body.

She had never realised the weakness of wanting or the power of passion until she knew Ross and felt her body stir at his touch. If he wanted her, she would run into his arms. Which just proved that she was as foolish and reckless as any other woman when it came to his charm, his charisma.

What was it about a rake that made so many women want him and believe they could turn him into a reliable and lasting lover?

Rakes didn't reform. Leopards didn't lose their spots. Any girl who allowed herself to fall deeply in love with Ross Harman could only expect a great deal of heart-ache in return . . .

CHAPTER SEVEN

Busy though they were on Paterson, Phyllida found that the days were long and empty without even the hope of seeing and talking to Ross. For only two of his patients were left on the ward, both convalescent. The houseman was keeping an eye on them prior to their discharge. There was nothing to bring Ross to Paterson and he was busy with patients on other wards.

He didn't try to see her. There were no more friendly notes left in the letter-rack of the Nurse' Home and no more invitations. Phyllida couldn't blame him. A man like Ross didn't have to waste his time on a first-year who kept blowing hot and cold.

Later that week, she heard through the grapevine that he had gone away for a few days. So had Georgy and the juniors gossiped and giggled over the likelihood that they were making the most of their opportunities out of sight and sound of Hartlake. The staff nurse had been seen leaving her flat with a suitcase and topcoat and Ross Harman's distinctive car had been parked outside, waiting.

Phyllida knew she had no right to be jealous. He was a free agent and could go where he pleased with whom he pleased. She just wished it was anyone but Georgy Knight!

It was much nicer on the ward without the staff nurse who always harried and hustled her and made no secret of her dislike and impatience. But Phyllida would have welcomed a dozen Georgy Knights in exchange for the assurance that she wasn't spending those off duty days and nights with Ross.

She was seeing a great deal of Kevin. She was so miserable that it didn't seem to matter if she stayed in with her books or tried to forget Ross in the company of a very different kind of man. She was cross with herself for wanting Ross—and found it impossible to want anyone else. Kevin was very patient, very considerate. It seemed that he might really be in love with her which was sad in one way and comforting in another. She was glad of his affection and his niceness. He might tease her prudishness, but he didn't get annoyed or try to force the issue. She liked him all the more for pretending to be content with the situation when he was a man like any other and obviously longed for a more intimate relationship.

But it was as much as Phyllida could do to return his kisses and stifle an instinctive protest at tentatively exploring caresses. She didn't want him to love her and it would be only fair to stop seeing him, she felt. But he insisted that he needed her and wouldn't make demands on her as long as they continued to meet. And, just now, she needed him and she supposed that, like any lover, he continued to hope that she would warm to him.

Georgy came back to work after her break looking just like the cat that had got at the cream, as one of the juniors declared. She had obviously enjoyed her off-duty days and was even pleasant to Phyllida which was a convincing sign that she had spent those days with Ross.

Phyllida tried not to hate the self-satisfied staff nurse—but it wasn't easy!

Ross was back, too. She didn't see him, but she heard that he was about the hospital, looking fit and rested and even more attractive—and she heard two of the nurses talking about him in the ward kitchen while they prepared the mid-morning drinks.

Intent on mixing a feed for a patient who was being fed by oesophageal tube after a pharyngectomy, Phyllida might have been virtually invisible, but she was straining both ears to catch every word as soon as she heard the mention of Ross Harman's name, quite unashamed of eavesdropping.

'Everyone says it's serious this time,' Mary Hammond declared firmly. 'He's going to marry our Georgy.'

Janet Burden wasn't very interested in the affairs of the handsome registrar, being newly-engaged to a medical student and much more concerned with her own. 'Even a rake can fall in love,' she said carelessly.

'No wonder Georgy's looking so pleased with herself and is being as nice as pie to everyone. I'd be pleased, too! He really is something else,' Mary sighed.

'Not my type.'

'Well, I fancy him,' Mary said bluntly. 'Not that he knows I'm on this planet. He almost walked through me just now! What is it about first-years that he just can't stand, I wonder?'

'We're the lowest of the low,' Janet told her cheerfully.

'No, really! Some of us aren't too bad to look at,' Mary said, preening herself with some justification for she was a pretty girl.

'It just isn't done. He *is* a registrar!'

'So's Ivor Maynard and he's going out with that first-year on Fleming.'

'If you mean Patti Parkin she's about thirty and nothing like a first-year!'

Phyllida bit back the immediate defence of poor Patti who was no more than twenty-three and a very lovely girl and deserved the attentions of a man as charming in his own way as Ross.

'It proves that we do exist for some of the senior doctors,' Mary insisted.

'Oh well. Perhaps a first-year turned Ross Harman down at some stage in his career as a Casanova and he bears a perpetual grudge against the species,' Janet suggested lightly.

'What girl would? He's an absolute dream. He only has to smile and I melt! Lucky Georgy!'

'You think it's true, then?' Janet asked curiously.

'Everyone says so,' Mary declared airily. 'All that's missing is the ring for her finger and he's supposed to be buying that this week!'

The clatter of the trolley as they trundled it out of the kitchen and into the ward drowned the other's girl's reply. Phyllida had heard too much, anyway—and she didn't like any of it.

She refused to believe the rumours. Without the slightest basis for the conviction, she just wouldn't accept that he was in love with Georgy Knight. She would know it in her bones! Nor did he have any intention of marrying the staff nurse whatever he might have encouraged her to think during their brief idyll in a country cottage. Georgy was making no secret of where she had been for those few days and she didn't seem to mind if the whole world knew that she had spent them with Ross Harman.

Phyllida went on with her work like the good nurse that she hoped to be one day. Personal feelings had no place on a busy ward, she told herself firmly. She couldn't run to the linen cupboard for a good cry every time her heart ached and it seemed that she would look in vain for Ross's broad shoulder however much she needed it. He had lost interest and probably forgotten that he had ever liked her. Well, she wasn't going to run after him, she thought proudly . . .

'Ross . . . !'

Forgetting pride and everything else but the need of her foolish heart, Phyllida hurried to catch him up as he paused, looked round at the eager sound of his name on her lips. She had been off duty that afternoon and she had been shopping in the West End. It was the purest chance that he happened to walk past the underground station entrance opposite the hospital just as she came up the steps, loaded with paper bags.

He smiled, not quite with his eyes. 'You look as though you've been having a spend-up,' he said lightly.

'Yes.' One of the parcels slipped from under her arm. She made a vain attempt to rescue it and lost another. She saw that his smile warmed and deepened in the dark eyes as he retrieved them. 'Thanks . . . how are you, Ross? I haven't seen you for ages.' She was a little breathless.

'I went away for a few days.'

'Oh?' She didn't mean to admit that she knew far too

much for comfort about those few days. 'Somewhere nice?'

'Dorset . . . near the New Forest. Some friends own a cottage in that part of the world. He's a doctor and she's a nurse . . . both ex-Hartlake.'

'Plenty of shop, then? I expect you enjoyed that,' she said carefully, wondering why he didn't seem to know that everyone at Hartlake had heard about his holiday with Georgy—and then wondering with a little alarm if he was just trying to spare her feelings. It would be dreadful if he realised just how she felt about his affair with the staff nurse.

'Very much,' he agreed, lying in his teeth. For all the time that he had been with Georgy, he had wanted the shy and reluctant Phyllida who was nothing like the women he had briefly cared about in the past.

It wasn't just her reluctance, her refusal to want him, although that was an undeniable challenge to a man like himself. Phyllida had character and warmth of heart and integrity as well as a rare sweetness. He liked and respected her as well as desired her with all the force of his strong sexuality.

He had tried to assuage the wanting in the arms of the beautiful and responsive and far from reluctant Georgy. He had taken her with hot-blooded and indifferent passion for he was not a man to refuse what was offered. But now, looking into Phyllida's candid eyes and sensing the generous warmth of her liking for him that owed nothing to sexual coquetry, he regretted the casual and meaningless intimacy that had left him strangely unsatisfied.

'We missed you on Paterson,' Phyllida said, greatly

daring and trying to make it sound as light and natural as possible.

'We . . . ?'

His dark eyes, amused, wouldn't allow her to look away and she realised that her tone hadn't been quite light enough. A little colour crept into her face. 'Oh, everyone. Staff, patients . . .'

'You, perhaps?'

He was direct. He was smiling, too, and her heart lifted. 'Yes, of course,' she said all in a rush. 'Yes, I missed you. Ross, I'm sorry I was so horrid the other evening . . .' She broke off as someone jostled her, knocking a parcel out of her hand and not pausing to apologise.

Stooping to pick it up, she had to make a hasty grab for a carrier bag whose handle suddenly broke under the weight of its contents. She didn't know whether to laugh or cry for she felt such an idiot, standing in the middle of the pavement surrounded by odds and ends of shopping, desperately trying to impress a man like Ross who could take his pick from dozens of prettier and more sophisticated and more capable girls than herself.

'Oh, dear . . .' she said, rather helplessly.

Ross laughed softly. 'Oh, Phyllida,' he said, very warm, her name an endearment. 'You'd better let me carry some of those things for you.'

He helped to collect the various items that were scattered over the pavement. Phyllida felt they were attracting a great deal of attention and thought he must wish that she hadn't caught sight of him.

'You weren't going my way,' she said, a little ruefully.

'I am now,' he returned cheerfully, untroubled by the

A special offer for readers of Mills & Boon

Four Mills & Boon Romances-FREE

We have chosen four Romances for you to enjoy FREE and without obligation as your special introduction to the Mills & Boon Reader Service.

Mills & Boon Romance
SEEN BY CANDLELIGHT
Anne Mather

Mills & Boon Romance
THE MARRIAGE OF CAROLINE LINDSAY
Margaret Rome

Mills & Boon Romance
THE IVORY CANE
Janet Dailey

Join the hundreds of readers enjoying Mills & Boon's Reader Service

Take these four free books and you will meet Ravena, about to marry a forbidding stranger to protect her beloved guardian from a terrible secret . . . Sabrina, tragically blinded in an accident, and afraid that the man she loves can offer no more than sympathy . . . Karen, forced to meet the husband she still loves two years after their divorce . . . Caroline, trapped by a misunderstanding that could lead her future husband to believe she deceived him.

Enjoy these moving love stories, and decide for yourself whether you would like to read more. If you would, the Mills & Boon Reader Service allows you to receive the very latest Mills & Boon titles hot from the presses every month, delivered to your door, post and packing free. There are many other exclusive advantages, too:

★ No commitment. You receive books for only as long as you want.
★ No hidden extra charges. Postage and packing is completely free.
★ Friendly, personal attention from Reader Service Editor Susan Welland. Why not call her now on 01-684 2141 if you have any queries?
★ FREE monthly newsletter crammed with competitions, knitting patterns,

recipes, bargain book offers, and exclusive special offers for you, your home and your friends.

THE FOUR FREE BOOKS ARE OUR SPECIAL GIFT TO YOU. THEY ARE YOURS TO KEEP WITHOUT ANY OBLIGATION TO BUY FURTHER BOOKS.

You have nothing to lose — and a whole world of romance to gain. See how the Reader Service can help you to enjoy Mills & Boon even more by filling in and posting the coupon today

Mills & Boon Reader Service, FREEPOST, P.O. Box 236, Croydon, Surrey CR9 9EL

FREE BOOKS CERTIFICATE

To: **Mills & Boon Reader Service, FREEPOST, P.O. Box 236, Croydon, Surrey CR9 9EL.**

Please send me, FREE AND WITHOUT OBLIGATION, the four Mills & Boon Romances illustrated above, and reserve a Reader Service Subscription for me. If I decide to subscribe I shall, from the beginning of the month following my free parcel of books, receive 6 new books each month for £5.70, post and packing free. If I decide not to subscribe, I shall write to you within 14 days. The free books are mine to keep in any case. I understand that I may cancel my subscription at any time simply by writing to you. I am over 18 years of age.

Name _____
(Please write in block capitals).
Address _____

_____

Town _____ County_____

Postcode _____   4D36
Send no money. Take no risks.   No stamp needed.

thought of the friend he had been on his way to meet in the bar of the Kingfisher. He was encouraged by the way she had called him, run after him, smiled into his eyes. He had his own methods for finding out what he wanted to know and it hadn't pleased him to discover that she was frequently in the company of Kevin Lawson. Jealousy was a novelty for Ross but he diagnosed it correctly. He caught her arm as she was about to step off the pavement in front of an oncoming car, shook his head at her in amused reproach. 'How did you get to be nineteen? You walk about with your eyes shut!'

She couldn't tell him that she was flustered by the unexpected encounter with him and thinking of very little but the magic in his smile. 'I'm nearly twenty,' she said quickly for his tone seemed to imply that he saw her as little more than a foolish, inept schoolgirl.

'Well, if you want to live to see your next birthday look both ways,' he advised dryly. 'Hartlake needs you!'

'Like a hole in the head,' she countered with a rueful smile. 'I'm the worst nurse ever to set foot on a hospital ward. Didn't you know?'

He smiled. 'Falling foul of Georgy again,' he said shrewdly. 'What did you do this time?'

She hesitated. 'Oh, tripped over a patient's foot,' she said airily.

He raised an eyebrow. 'That doesn't sound a very terrible crime.'

'I was carrying a bowl of washing water and most of it went over Georgy. She thought I did it on purpose, of course.'

'I rather think my sympathies are with Georgy,' he said, eyes twinkling.

She sighed. 'I thought they might be.' They had reached the door of the Nurses' Home and she was conscious of a few curious glances from other nurses on their way in and out of the building. She turned to take her parcels from him. 'Thanks. I'm really grateful. You keep coming to my rescue.'

She wondered if she had the courage to ask if they might meet for a drink that evening. Lots of girls took the initiative these days when they liked a man, after all. It had never been possible for someone as shy as herself. But she had never wanted any man as much as she wanted Ross and she desperately wished him to think of her as an attractive woman instead of just an accident-prone junior.

'It's time you came to my rescue,' he told her lightly. 'I've some friends coming to supper this evening and I need someone to cook the steaks while I toss the salad. How about helping me out?'

Phyllida was surprised and delighted. She didn't know why he persisted in being so nice to her but she reminded herself sternly not to attach too much importance to it. After all, she was no competition for the beautiful and very sexy Georgy Knight. Unless Georgy was hopeless at cooking steaks . . .

'I'd love to,' she said promptly.

'That's better,' he approved with dancing eyes and a smile in their depths that tilted her heart. 'That's the kind of response I expect from my women and it's time you ran out of negatives.'

Phyllida smiled but the reminder of the many girls in his past seemed to emphasise his lack of sexual intent where she was concerned. It was a blow to any girl's ego.

At the same time, she supposed it was a compliment that he sought her company for its own sake . . .

She dithered for some time over what to wear and finally settled for a black skirt with colourful flowers of appliqued velvet and a filmy black blouse with flowing, loose sleeves and a scoop neckline that exposed the slight swell of her breasts. She felt that she looked elegant as well as alluring—even if it was a waste of time!

Ross didn't comment as he handed her into his car, but she fancied there was a glow of appreciation in his eyes and didn't his hand linger just a fraction on her arm? Sitting beside him as he drove, she tried not to notice the unmistakable hint of a woman's perfume. Georgy Knight—or some other girl? It was none of her business, she told herself firmly, closing her mind to the image of other women in his arms. He could have invited any of a dozen girls to play hostess for him that evening. He had chosen her. What more did she want?

Glancing at that handsome profile as he manoeuvred the car through a stream of traffic on the way to his flat, Phyllida melted with longing and knew that she wanted much more than he would ever give. But she also knew that she would take whatever came her way and be grateful.

Ross took a hand from the wheel and reached for one of the hands that lay loosely linked in her lap. 'I have a confession to make,' he said lightly. 'I've lured you to my flat on false pretences—although I swear I didn't know it at the time. My friends can't make it, after all. Julie has come down with a flu bug. I could have phoned you but I didn't see why you should be cheated out of your supper—even if you do have to cook it yourself!'

Her heart gave a little jump that was more excitement than apprehension at the thought of spending the entire evening alone with him but she doubted if he had seduction in mind. He was too casual, too relaxed. There wasn't the least hint of sexual tension in his attitude. He didn't seem to know that her body leaped to life at his merest touch and that she yearned desperately for the lovemaking he bestowed so readily on every other woman but herself.

'That's all right,' she assured him. 'You have to eat, too, after all—and I like cooking. It would be a shame to waste the steaks.'

She was so matter-of-fact that Ross was baffled by her indifference to the potent sexuality that had won him so many other women. She just didn't want to know, he thought wryly. It didn't seem to cross her mind that the evening might end very satisfactorily in each other's arms. He didn't think she was frigid. Just un-awakened . . .

Phyllida was very interested in seeing how and where he lived. She suspected that it would be very different from Kevin's dingy bed-sitter. She was right. For Ross wasn't financially dependent on his salary as a registrar in a teaching hospital. He could well afford the luxurious flat in a modern block beside the Thames.

It was very much a bachelor pad and she was surprised. There had been so many women in and out of his life that she had expected some result of their influence, some feminine touches about his home. There were none.

He went into the kitchen to take steaks from the fridge and instal some wine to cool and Phyllida took the opportunity to look at his books, his pictures, his extensive collection of records and the expensive stereo equipment.

Ross returned to the living-room. He paused by the door to study her as she sorted through his record albums. She was slim and lovely and very appealing. She was unconsciously alluring, too, stirring his senses in that sexy black outfit that set off her beautiful skin and the gold glints in her chestnut curls. The low cut of the flimsy blouse hinted at the loveliness of taut, exciting breasts that thrust against the filmy stuff with a tantalising effect, setting the hot blood coursing swiftly through his veins.

She looked so young that it was something of a shock to him. Of course, she was very young . . . not yet twenty. Too young and too innocent, he thought ruefully. He would need to keep a tight rein on the longing that threatened to overwhelm him. He mustn't rush her, mustn't alarm her. It might take weeks of subtle persuasion before she came into his arms with the warm and willing response that he ached to know. He wanted her more than any woman he had ever known.

'Anything you'd like to hear?' he asked lightly, crossing the room to her side.

Phyllida smiled and held out a favourite. 'I like this one.'

He glanced at the label. 'Mood music. We have similar tastes.' He switched on the stereo and placed the record on the turntable. Music filled the room, loud. He turned it low.

He was disturbingly close and much too attractive. Phyllida thought he must surely hear the pounding of her heart and sense the growing need in her body. He looked down at her, smiled . . . and impulsively she moved into him and put her arms about him, knowing it was foolish, reckless, inviting rebuff—or, worse, the loveless love-making of a rake who was also an opportunist.

He didn't kiss her and she didn't dare to kiss him. She had probably gone too far as it was! He only held her, his cheek hard against her head. Phyllida could feel the thump of his heart, the quick rise and fall of his chest. Absurdly, she found that she was counting respirations and she pulled herself up short. How stupid to be thinking like a nurse when she was feeling like a woman, aware of him with every quickened pulse, every wave of the desire that he evoked without even trying.

Ross stood rigid, fighting temptation with all his might. It took all his self-control to keep his body from betraying the instinctive, leaping throb of desire. The fierce flame was almost frightening in its intensity. There had been so many women, most of them forgotten. Not one had consumed him with this kind of eager yet oddly tender wanting.

He held her, not daring to kiss her, filled with a yearning that he hesitated to betray. For she had turned into his arms so trustingly, of her own accord, surprising him with that generous gesture of affection—and Ross didn't want to think that she might be near to loving him. For that meant that he would have to end their rela-tionship before it had properly begun.

For the first time, he hesitated to take what a woman offered—and wished that he didn't want her so much that it was damnably hard to refuse, to turn away . . .

The doorbell buzzed abruptly, shattering the moment. They were both thankful—for very different reasons.

Phyllida drew away, not meeting his eyes. She had embarrassed and disconcerted him. She wanted to sink through the floor with the humiliation of having hurled herself at a man who didn't want her at all. 'I guess your friends have arrived, after all.'

'Possibly . . .' He moved towards the door.

Phyllida didn't see that he was trembling. She only saw that he hurried almost thankfully to admit his friends. He was nicer than anyone knew, she thought heavily. He hadn't recoiled from her although it was obvious that he had been dismayed. Nor had he taken prompt advantage of one more girl who was silly enough to fall head over heels for his looks and his charm and his physical attractions.

It wasn't his friends. It was a neighbour who habitually went out without his door-key and left a spare with Ross for such an eventuality. He came in for a drink and stayed for two, talking interminably and gazing at Phyllida with blatant admiration and interest.

Ross bore with him because he knew that Mark's interruption had given Phyllida the time she needed. He was too experienced not to know what she had felt when she stood in his arms. He had sensed the wanting that had fired his own and he was sure that he could have swept her into bed without a murmur of protest—and heaven knew he had been tempted!

But while girls like Georgy knew exactly what they were doing when they invited a man to make love to them, Phyllida had simply been following an impulse and he wouldn't have liked himself very much if he'd taken advantage of her innocence and warmth of heart, he thought wryly.

And she might have hated him when passion cooled . . .

CHAPTER EIGHT

MARK finally took his leave, reluctantly. Ross closed the door firmly on his talkative friend and went back to Phyllida. She stood by the big window with its panoramic view of the river and across London to St Paul's. It was quite a spectacular show in the setting sun and one of the reasons why he had bought this flat.

'Sorry about that . . . he's a decent chap but his timing is terrible,' he said, deliberately light because he wanted to ease her obvious embarrassment. He doubted if she was in the habit of casting out lures and it must have been very disconcerting for her that he had resisted the invitation in her embrace.

'So's mine,' she said with rueful candour. There was little point in pretending that she hadn't put her arms round him and been rebuffed. 'Talk about fools rushing in . . .'

His heart smote him. Trying to protect her, he had only succeeded in hurting her. 'You beat me to it by half a second,' he said swiftly, smiling.

She didn't believe him. 'Oh, I'm a brazen hussy,' she said brightly, making light of disappointment and wounded pride as best she could.

He touched his hand to her soft cheek. 'You're very sweet,' he said quietly. 'I'm very fond of you . . .'

She thought that might be true—and wondered why it

wasn't nearly enough. 'I wish you wouldn't be so nice when you're supposed to be a horrid, heartless rake,' she said in mock scolding. 'It confuses me!'

'And that isn't difficult,' he returned, teasing her gently.

She laughed to please him. 'No, it isn't!'

He looked down at her, suddenly very much in earnest. 'Don't be misled, Phyllida. I *am* a heartless rake. So think twice about encouraging me to make love to you unless you really know where it leads. A man like me lives by a maxim you won't like—*bed them, don't wed them.*'

Her face flamed. She moved away from him, sick at heart and trying not to show it. It was an unmistakable warning and she wished that she could exclaim proudly and with truth that the thought of marrying him had never entered her head.

She said carefully: 'You don't have to spell it out for me, Ross. I know you don't want me.'

His eyes narrowed abruptly. 'What makes you think so?'

She smiled wryly. 'I'm not exciting. Not like Georgy . . .'

'Nothing like Georgy! Don't ever try to be!' he said emphatically. 'I like you just the way you are—and that's enough excitement for any man. It takes me all my time to keep my hands off you!'

Phyllida raised a startled, incredulous face. 'You're just being kind . . .' she began defensively.

'Kind! For God's sake, Phyllida! What do I have to do to convince you?' he demanded, torn between anger and tender amusement at her innocence.

Searching his eyes, still unsure, her heart began to pound. Suddenly she smiled, unaware of the sweet spontaneity that had captivated him when he first saw it. 'You could k-kiss me,' she suggested with the slightest of heart-catching stammers.

Ross chuckled, delighted. 'That hadn't occurred to me, of course,' he said, very dry. He bent his head and heard the little sighing catch of her breath as their lips met. He drew her into his arms, suddenly urgent.

His kiss was all that she had dreamed and more, transporting her to a kind of heaven. She clung to him, lost in the magic, weak with wanting and helpless before the tidal wave of desire that he knew just how to evoke with his warm lips and his hands on her body.

Abruptly, he put her away from him, a rueful expression in his dark eyes, caring more for her inexperience than his own sensual satisfaction. 'You're too much temptation,' he said with longing.

Phyllida no longer felt that the wanting was all on her side. His ardour and his urgency, so evident in that lean, hard body and the way he had kissed her, was greater than her own for he knew the ecstasy to be found in sexual communion and she was still a stranger to its mysteries. She was suddenly impatient with virginity. She wanted to *know*. She loved him and she wanted to lie in his arms and know the power and the glory. The power of passion and the glory of giving for his delight and her own. In his arms, she would gladly step over the threshold between unknowing maidenhood and fulfilled womanhood.

She put her arms about his neck and leaned against him. 'Are you turning me down?' she said softly, provocatively. 'That doesn't sound like the Ross Harman I know and love.'

He tensed at the words for all their easy lightness and Phyllida knew that she had made a mistake.

'Phyllida,' he said achingly, torn between wanting and wisdom. The small, thrusting breasts were a torment to his sexuality. The slender body, so close and so yielding, excited him beyond bearing. The clamouring need was driving him to the edge of control and soon he wouldn't give a damn for anything but taking her in fierce and hungry passion. 'The way I feel about you right now has nothing to do with love.'

A lesser man might have pretended. He could not and she loved him all the more for that. She kissed him, lips very sweet. 'Just want me . . . oh, Ross, just want me!' she sighed, little flames of fire darting in all the secret places of her vulnerable, virgin body.

He took her small face in both his hands and looked long and searching into the deep blue eyes and she looked back at him, smiling, unashamed and unafraid. He did not mean to love any woman but he felt that he was very near to loving her in that moment. He kissed her with a gentle passion so that he wouldn't shatter the willing mood.

She trembled as he drew her down to the wide bed and into his eager embrace, his kiss becoming deeper and more demanding, his hand sliding beneath the thin blouse to curve about her breast. She sighed against his lips as the warm, sensual caresses sent ripples of delight through her body. The warmth and generosity of her response was unexpected and delightful, enchanting and exciting him.

He undressed her with reverent hands. She heard the quick catch of his breath at her nude loveliness and she was glad that her body pleased him. He bent his head to kiss her bare breasts, to nuzzle the taut nipples with sensual lips and she put her arms about him to draw him down to her, eager and impatient.

Ross resisted, wiser than she was, concerned for her innocence and inexperience. Just now, he was too near the ultimate ecstasy and he was thankful for the maturity and skill that enabled him to hold back the mounting passion so that he would not disappoint her. Instead, he made sensual, skilful love to her with his kisses and the strong, sweeping caresses, knowing just how to please and delight and coax her towards the final surrender . . .

He ignored the first shrill summons of the telephone, refusing to let it break the spell for all the instinct and training of a doctor who responded automatically to the sound.

Phyllida stirred in his arms, sighed.

His arms tightened about her, his lips moved against the sweet, intoxicating mouth that kissed him as no woman had ever kissed him before, with all her generous, giving and very loving heart.

The sound of the telephone was strident and insistent and persistent. Phyllida eased herself away from the promise of enchantment. 'Ross . . .'

'Oh, hell!' He kissed her again, quick and hard . . . and then he reached to lift the receiver, reluctant but compelled by the knowledge that even off-duty he was always on call in an emergency.

Phyllida lay, very tense, struggling with the wild throb of desire and aware of him in every fibre of her being, while he talked briefly and brusquely into the telephone. He named no names but she knew it was Georgy and she thought how delighted the staff nurse would be to know that she had shattered the spell of their mutual enchantment.

The call only lasted a few moments and he was so cold, so curt that she wondered if he knew that his manner must arouse Georgy's suspicions—and if he cared.

But it gave her time to fill with sick dismay at the realisation that she was lying where too many girls had lain before her . . . in his bed, in his sensual and uncaring arms, eager to give without counting the cost because she had fallen headlong in love with a man who would never love her.

Ross turned back to her with a murmur of rueful apology and obvious intent in the way he reached to take her into his arms. She held him at bay with both small hands against his hard chest. 'No . . .'

He mentally consigned Georgy to the depths. 'It's too late to say no, Phyllida,' he said gently, nuzzling her slender neck with his lips. 'We want each other too much and there's a point of no return. It's only one step to being lovers and several steps back to being friends.'

She held him, his dark head on her breast, her fingers twining in the crisp curls that clung to her touch as she had always known they would. Against all her instincts, she struggled to safeguard herself from certain heartache and humiliation.

'That was Georgy,' she said carefully.

'Yes.'

She heard the impatience in his tone, sensed it in the sudden tension of his body against her own. 'Don't you feel that you owe her anything?' she asked quietly, driven by the returning caution of a level-headed and responsible girl to disappoint him and hurt herself.

'For God's sake! What has Georgy to say to anything where you and I are concerned? She doesn't own me.'

'But you're still lovers.' She tried to keep her tone light. She wanted to burst into tears at the dreadful pain and anguish that almost tore her into pieces at the thought of Georgy or any other girl in his embrace.

'I took her because I wanted you,' he said roughly. 'You don't understand that, of course. Women never do. But it's the truth, Phyllida. You kept me at arms' length and she was willing. That's all it meant.'

She touched her lips to his dark hair. She *didn't* understand but she believed that the affair with Georgy meant very little. 'I'm not jealous . . . not really.'

And it wasn't jealously. Just the heartache of knowing that she was no more than a passing fancy like Georgy— and all the others.

'You don't need to be,' he told her warmly. 'There's never been anyone quite like you. You're special . . .' He reached for her and kissed her with rising need. But the warm and willing lips had turned cool, although she returned his kiss.

He began to make slow, sensuous love to her all over again. Phyllida checked him with her hands and the stiffening of her body. 'Don't, Ross . . .'

He sighed. 'It's dangerous to blow hot and cold with a man like me,' he warned, meaning it. 'I might insist on taking what you change your mind about giving.' She drew herself out of his arms. He pulled her back, angry. 'I'm not joking!'

Phyllida turned impulsively into his arms and embraced him and touched her lips to the stern, unsmiling mouth. It was silent surrender. She loved him. She didn't want to disappoint him. Her body was still tingling and throbbing with unfulfilled longing, even if her heart was no longer in the lovemaking that was only sexual gratification for him.

Swept beyond all control by that sweet and intoxicating yielding, he took her on a storm of passion that left them both breathless and shaken and spent.

It was a hollow victory for Ross, despising himself. Sexual conquest for its own sake of a girl he should have continued to protect from her own impetuous generosity. Somehow it hadn't been enough that he wanted her so desperately. Somehow her readiness to receive him as a lover had been too much.

It had been wonder such as she had never expected, an incredible new world of wonder, and Phyllida clung to him, euphoric, a wealth of loving words trembling on her lips. She checked them because she knew he would think that she was carried away by her emotions, but she had loved him for some time. She had loved him before she knew it and she would always love him.

He was too silent, too still, troubling her for she sensed that he did not share her golden content in the aftermath of lovemaking. She leaned on her elbow to look at him and saw that his innermost thoughts and feelings were hidden to her. She looked into the eyes of a stranger and her heart contracted with sudden fear. 'What is it?' she asked carefully. 'What's wrong?'

'All of it,' he said, curt. 'You're too involved and I'm not involved enough—and don't mean to be!' He saw that she flinched and forced himself to continue. It was better to hurt her a little now than maybe break her generous heart in the long run. 'I know myself better than you do, Phyllida. It would take a miracle to change me from the man I am.'

'Oh, Ross,' she murmured achingly, pressing her face against his bare shoulder, kissing the warm flesh. 'Maybe I believe in miracles . . .'

He put a hand to her head and cradled it with a tenderness that belied the brutality of what he was about to do to her. 'I don't want you regretting that you ever knew me. So it stops, here and now—and if I'd known how different you are to most girls, it would never have started!' he said bluntly.

Her heart shrank from the implication of the words. 'Does that mean that you don't want to see me again?' she asked shakily.

'That's right.' He was cool, indifferent.

Had she been such a disappointment? She was too proud to ask—and suddenly angry that the precious intimacy should mean so little to him. She drew away from him. 'So it's true what everyone says about you!' she said bitterly. 'You *are* heartless! And quite ruthless! And only interested in one thing until you get it!'

He smiled wryly. 'I did warn you.'

'Yes. You warned me and I didn't want to believe that you could be so cold-blooded.'

He raised an amused eyebrow. 'I don't think you could call me cold-blooded, Phyllida.'

She reached for her clothes. 'The way you talked to Georgy on the 'phone should have told me the kind of man you are,' she said heavily. 'You've finished with her, too, haven't you? Only she doesn't know it yet! Letting her down lightly, Ross? You might have done the same for me!' Taking her clothes, she fled to the bathroom, slammed and locked the door.

She dressed hastily, trying not to remember with what caressing tenderness he had removed those same clothes. She thrust her tumbled hair back from her face with trembling hands, trying not to think how much she loved him and how dreadful the future was going to be without him.

She was shattered but she couldn't cry. Some things went too deep for tears. Very pale but composed, she emerged from the bathroom to find that he had dressed and was waiting for her in the living-room.

She looked at him with guarded eyes. 'We forgot the steaks,' she said with a courageous attempt at a smile. Perhaps if he thought she was as light-hearted as himself at loving, he wouldn't thrust her out of his life so abruptly. He just didn't want to be loved with all the demands it might make on him.

The look in her eyes tore unexpectedly at his heart. He held out his arms and she ran into them, thankful. Ross held her, lips against the soft hair, wishing she didn't make it so hard for him to end it. But he had to protect her from a man like himself and he wished he could turn back the clock and give back what he had taken from her. For one day, when she found a man who really merited her love and her trust and wanted to marry her, she would think of him with hate.

'I didn't mean to make love to you,' he said, low, regretful. 'I tried so hard to resist temptation.'

'I know.' Her voice was muffled.

'I'm not the man for you, Phyllida. The way you feel will pass and you'll be grateful that I didn't let you throw away any more of your life on someone like me.'

'I want you,' she said, voice shaking, forgetting all about pride and common-sense and self-respect. They didn't do much for an aching heart, after all. They couldn't alter what had happened. 'I don't want it to end . . .' He silenced her with his lips and the unmistakable finality in that gentle kiss struck at the very core of her being. She pushed him away, despairing. 'You haven't any heart,' she said, wondering just how many girls had said it before her. 'You just don't care!'

Ross cared more than she knew. But he wasn't going to let a sweet and lovely girl waste herself on a worthless rake.

He reached for her velvet coat. 'I'll take you home.'

'No. I'll get a taxi.' Her chin tilted. Suddenly she had discovered the remnants of her pride. She took her coat from his hand. 'You needn't feel that you owe me anything, Ross—any more than any of the others. If it wasn't you it would have been someone else very soon. Probably Kevin Lawson.' She turned to the door. 'At least he'd have fed me. He's a very good cook,' she added brightly.

'Phyllida . . .' He moved after her, took her arm.

She took off his hand. 'Please . . . don't touch me,' she said tensely, heart hammering so hard that she felt sick and breathless. 'Don't ever—touch me again!'

'I'm driving you back to Hartlake, Phyllida. It's the least I can do.'

'No. Your car reeks of someone else's scent. I should be sick,' she told him bluntly, meaning it.

'Then I'll take you by taxi.'

'I can take myself. I'm not a child or an idiot whatever you may think! No . . . don't come down with me. I can even cope with a lift, surprising though it may seem!'

She managed to keep back the tears until the closing doors concealed her from his view. Then they came, blinding and choking her and doing nothing at all to ease the pain that radiated all over her from somewhere in the region of her heart. She had to pull herself together as the lift reached the ground floor. She hurried across the vestibule and out to the street and hailed a passing taxi with relief. Sinking into the back seat, she buried her face in her hands.

How was she going to meet him on the ward, however briefly and unimportantly, without feeling the burn of heartache and humiliation, without remembering? How could she stay at Hartlake within sight and sound of a man who had taken her in swift and ecstatic passion and then casually decided that she had nothing more to offer and that he didn't want to see her again?

She had asked for it, of course. She had let him see that she liked him, run after him, thrown herself at him with unmistakable wanting—and he was an opportunist. A rake without heart or conscience.

He had treated her like a one-night stand, a casual pick-up. He had used her and cheapened her. She had been just another conquest and he'd made no effort to pretend that she was anything more once the lovemaking was over.

Only Kate was in the flat when Phyllida reached it, wild-eyed and white-faced and unaware of it. Kate took one look at her friend's stricken face and knew the hell she was going through because she had been there herself. It did come to an end and there was a new kind of happiness to be found on the other side of a very dark tunnel, she had discovered. But who knew that or believed it when one's world first fell about one's ears?

Caring and concerned and much too sensitive to ask questions or to show that she even noticed the obvious distress, Kate busied herself with making tea in the pretence that she needed it after an evening with textbooks and notebooks.

Phyllida was grateful for the hot tea but she couldn't face the toasted sandwich that Kate set thoughtfully in front of her. She didn't think that she would ever want to eat again. She wondered if her heart would ever stop aching. She thought of girls in Victorian times who had gone into a decline and quietly died after a disappointment in love and she understood the bleak feeling that nothing mattered any more.

She was all heart but she was not entirely foolish and she told herself firmly that no one really died of a broken heart. Victorian girls had simply become consumptive through self-neglect. She hoped she had too much sense to think it was really the end of all her hopes and dreams of happiness because she had fallen in love with a man who didn't love her. It just felt that way for the moment.

But she had come to Hartlake to be a nurse and not to lose her heart to the first attractive man who took her fancy, she rebuked herself sternly. It was only a fancy and it would probably die a natural death if she didn't foster it with a great deal of nonsense about being lastingly in love.

The best thing she could do was to devote herself to

being a much better nurse who didn't drop things and fall over things and cause general chaos on the ward and draw too much attention to herself. Ross would never have noticed her at all if she hadn't earned a reputation for being hopelessly accident-prone and a constant thorn in Georgy Knight's side. For everyone knew that he had no time for first-year nurses as a rule.

She could have done without the accolade of being the exception . . .

CHAPTER NINE

SISTER Hamilton gathered her nurses about the ward desk for Report. She ran through it briskly, but with careful attention to detail, allocating tasks and acquainting them of ward changes.

Phyllida tried to pay attention, but her thoughts kept slipping away from matters that did not concern a very junior nurse who would spend most of her day on routine chores.

She had spent a sleepless night, not so much in regretting what had happened but in fretting for the might-have-been. Now she was dreading an encounter with Ross and hoping that nothing would bring him to the ward that day. She needed time to be able to face him without remembering too vividly the touch of his hands on her body, the ecstasy they had shared, the heartbreak that had tarnished the golden memory of sexual delight in the arms of the man she loved.

She tried not to think how much she loved him. She tried not to feel that she would always love him when it would not bring her the slightest happiness or any promise for the future. And she tried not to look round instinctively every time that the ward doors swung to and fro as someone came in or went out.

'. . . Miss Hastings and Mrs Farmer have had their pre-meds. Miss Maitland is going down to X-Ray for a pyelograph this morning. Miss Keith is to have a lumbar puncture. We are admitting Mrs Powell for gall bladder removal, Miss Marshall for a mastectomy and Mrs Harvey for a laparotomy. Miss Nelson, Mrs David and Mrs Carmichael are going home.' Sister looked up, smiled. 'Thank you, Nurses.'

As they rose and hurried away to begin the day's routine, she called Phyllida back to the desk. She had noted the unusual pallor, the shadows beneath very blue eyes, the tension that showed itself in her marked in-attentiveness and the stiffening every time that the ward doors opened or closed.

'Are you well, Nurse Sims?' She had a fondness for this well-meaning junior who tried too hard to be an asset to the ward.

'Yes, thank you, Sister.' Phyllida was wary. If Sister Hamilton had noticed that something was wrong then so would Ross if they met too soon. And she didn't want him to realise how badly he had hurt her. It would be a sure betrayal that she loved him.

'*You're too involved . . .*' he had said, with truth, but he didn't seem to know that it was much too late for her to draw back from loving. He thought she could stop caring if they stopped meeting!

'*I don't mean to get involved,*' he had told her firmly and his heart would remain untouched by her or any other girl because that was the way he wanted it.

Men were so reluctant to give too much of themselves to any relationship and they were deft at handling such situations. Ross was probably more skilled than most through long experience. A woman didn't seem to have much say in the matter when it came to loving, Phyllida thought ruefully. She just followed her destiny . . .

'Quite well?' Sister Hamilton persisted.

'Yes, Sister.'

'Something on your mind, perhaps. A family upset or a quarrel with the boy-friend?' The tone was gentle, concerned. The smooth running of the ward was dependent to some extent on the mental attitude of the staff. Anxiety about personal affairs could affect a nurse's work to the detriment of the patients.

Phyllida shook her head. 'No, Sister.' Ross could scarcely be described as a boy-friend!

'Then I suspect that you've been working too hard. I know you're a very conscientious nurse and want to do well. But you mustn't sit up to all hours with your books and make yourself ill or I shall have to speak to Home Sister about you!'

'Yes, Sister.'

'You may go and help Nurse Buckley with the drugs round. But make sure that you have a break from studying this evening, Nurse. Go out with your friends and enjoy yourself. You're a long way yet from first-year exams and all work and no play makes Phyl dull and heavy-eyed and inattentive to Report,' she added with a smile and a twinkle in her eyes.

Phyllida hurried away, thinking how lucky they were on Paterson to have a ward sister who cared about her nurses as well as the patients. Even a rebuke was given gently and with humour so that it stayed in the mind. She knew she would be careful not to let her thoughts stray again during Report. Sister Hamilton, like the marvellous nurse and efficient administrator that she was, never missed a thing!

Later that morning, she was sent to Pharmacy with a list of drugs urgently required for the ward. It was a bright and sunny day and Phyllida took a short cut across the gardens, a pleasant square that was presided over by a statue of Sir Henry Hartlake, founder of the famous teaching hospital. The benevolent smile of the stout philanthropist seemed to embrace all those who hurried along the paved paths between one tall building and another. Nurses in the traditional and well-known uniform, doctors and medical students in their white coats, radiographers and physiotherapists and phlebotomists and lab technicians in their short coats of different colours, porters in their distinctive grey, patients and relatives and other visitors to Hartlake.

Some very new nurses from the Preliminary Training School, known as Pets to the medical students, were grouped on the lawn with their books and that air of anxiety that hinted at lack of confidence, enjoying a short break from lectures and practical work with Sister Tutors.

It was not so long since Phyllida had been just as green, just as apprehensive about the future and worried by unfamiliar names of bones and muscles and nerves, just as nervous of nursing real people in place of the PTS dolls. Joe and Jane were lifesize and lifelike, but they didn't bruise if they fell out of bed during a blanket bath or scald if they were given a too-hot poultice or complain if a bandage was applied too tightly, cutting off circulation.

Phyllida had just reached Sir Henry's statue and was tempted to sit in the sun for a few moments on the wooden seat that encircled its base when she saw Ross, striding towards her with white coat flying and a pur-poseful look in his dark eyes.

She almost fled so that they wouldn't meet. But, being Phyllida, she stood her ground, chin tilted and eyes sparkling with a hint of militant pride. She might be very much in love, but she was also very angry that he had taken and used and discarded her like all the other women he had known. Foolishly, she had hoped that she was different, more important. He had encouraged her to think so, after all. '*You're special*', he had said, warm and softly persuasive.

Ross saw her and checked, not too sure of what to say to her or how she felt about him this morning. As soon as the lift swept her from sight, he had known that he didn't want to lose the generous warmth and sweetness that was Phyllida. He had headed for the stairs to catch her before she could leave the building—and cursed the departing taxi, never available in an emergency and cruising too conveniently at hand on occasions such as this one!

He might have leaped into his car and followed, intercepting her at the door of the Nurses' Home. But discretion and the conviction that they both needed time to think had taken him back to his flat where the uneaten steaks and rumpled bed did nothing to raise his spirits—or his opinion of himself!

Despising himself, and a little anxious that she might not easily forgive, Ross had scarcely slept. He had been haunted by the thought of her in his arms, too. So sweet her lips, so warm and yielding the lovely body. Even more disturbing for a man like him, such enchantment in the eyes and smile and lilting voice that it threatened the self-sufficiency and the independence and the freedom that he had always valued so much.

Now, meeting the beautiful blue eyes, he saw that they were cold with contempt. He had always been a care-for-nobody but suddenly he cared that she should think well of him although he knew that she had no reason to do so.

'Phyllida,' he said, concerned, seeing that every vestige of colour had drained from the small face at sight of him. 'How are you . . . ?' Such trite, inadequate words. Such unwelcome awkwardness between two people who had so recently lain in each other's arms as lovers . . . and now couldn't even be friends, he realised with regret.

'Fine.' Her tone was cool, brittle. 'And in a hurry.'

He put a hand on her arm as she was about to brush past him. 'Just a minute . . .' She sent him such a blistering look that his hand fell away. He was dismayed. It seemed that she had meant those furious words of the previous night. His touch was no longer welcome, however light, not even in casual and very ordinary friendliness. 'I know what you must think of me,' he said quietly. 'I just want to say that I'm really sorry for what happened last night.'

'But I asked for it, didn't I?' Phyllida's smile was bleak. 'And you're the kind to take what you can and then despise the girl for giving. I was a fool to forget it and to think you were worth bothering about. At least I'm not so stupid that I can't learn from my mistakes!'

She left him, walking quickly in her haste to get away from him. Ross looked after her, frowning, more shaken than he cared to admit and just a little angry that she wouldn't allow him to make amends. Then, aware of curious glances, he went on his way.

She would come round, he told himself. Women always did. His charm had never failed him yet and it didn't seem likely that Phyllida could thrust him out of her life without a backward glance.

But she might, he thought wryly, confidence flagging. He just wasn't at all sure about Phyllida. She had a lot of spirit, a lot of character, an integrity that he had found in very few of her sex and he was afraid that she might resolve to forget all about him—and do just that!

There were other men in her life—Kevin Lawson for one. Why should he suppose that he meant more to her than the others? Just because a virgin went to bed with a man she found attractive, did that give the man the right to assume that she really cared for him? She was young and impulsive and very generous. That didn't mean she was in love with him.

When it came to Phyllida, Ross wasn't at all confident of getting what he wanted. And for the first time in his life, he discovered that the wanting wasn't just sexually motivated . . .

When Phyllida got back to Paterson from Pharmacy, she didn't need to catch a glimpse of Ross to know that he was on the ward. One glance at Georgy Knight's bright eyes and radiant smile told its own story.

Remembering the brusque way that he had spoken to the staff nurse on the telephone, a quite unmistakable brush-off from a man involved with someone else at the time, she was surprised. But perhaps he had offered an apology and a convincing explanation. Or Georgy, like so many women, was prepared to put up with anything rather than lose him.

Two of the new admissions, the gall bladder and the laparotomy, were Professor Wilson's patients . . . As his registrar, Ross would probably do both operations. In any case, it was his responsibility to examine them on admission and explain the proposed surgery. He had the confident, reassuring manner of the skilled and sensitive surgeon and both patients, naturally rather apprehensive, felt more relaxed after he had talked to them. He encouraged questions and provided comprehensive answers and told them what to expect. In Mrs Harvey's case, an investigatory abdominal operation, no one knew quite what to expect but Ross believed in being cheerful and optimistic. She was a sensible woman who had consulted her GP at the first signs of trouble and if it proved to be a malign tumour, Ross had every confidence that it would be operable. Early detection and radium therapy meant that cancer was no longer the scourge that few people even dared to talk about and he was thankful that the public were being educated to seek advice and, in many cases, reassurance in good time.

While he discussed both cases with Sister, he was conscious of Phyllida's gentle coaxing of a reluctant post-operative patient to put her feet to the floor and walk the first few steps. With an arm about the woman's ample waist, half-supporting her, she encouraged and persuaded and praised with seemingly genuine interest and concern. The mark of a promising nurse, he thought.

Sister Hamilton saw that the surgeon's eyes were on the pretty first-year with something more than his usual flirtatious interest in their depths. She felt a momentary surprise—and dismissed it. Phyllida Sims was a nice child, but much too young to attract a man like Ross Harman. Georgy Knight was much more his style and everyone knew just what was going on between them, she thought dryly.

'. . . the usual tests and X-rays, of course, Sister. My boss will be round to see both patients tomorrow. Mrs Powell should be simple removal with no complications and I'm expecting her to be well enough for discharge in ten days. We'll know more about Mrs Harvey's prognosis after we've had a look round.' Ross glanced at his watch . . . and again at Phyllida, carefully easing the big woman back against her pillows to rest after the brief exercise. 'I'll be back later to take some blood from Mrs Harvey for matching. I'm due in Outpatients.'

Sister Hamilton briefly basked in the warmth of his very attractive smile—and then he went, pushing through the swing doors, a man in a hurry. She had known him too long and too well to be vulnerable to his brand of charm but she understood why so many of her very junior nurses sighed over him. In vain, of course. Ross Harman hadn't dated a first-year since his medical student days.

She saw that he had left a folder on her desk, full of papers that he would no doubt need for his clinic in Outpatients. She beckoned to the nearest unoccupied nurse.

'Nurse Sims, run after Mr Harman with these papers—quickly! He's on his way to Outpatients!'

Phyllida couldn't refuse. A nurse had to obey instructions without question or hesitation, she reminded herself. But it went against the grain to run after Ross for any reason at all!

Not that a nurse was expected to run except in cases of fire, or haemmorhage, or cardiac arrest, of course. Sister had only been using a figure of speech. Phyllida took the folder and thrust through the ward doors and hurried along the corridor to the lifts. One of them was on its way down and Ross had probably taken it to the ground floor. She headed for the staircase rather than wait for the other lift.

Looking down the stairwell as she hurried down the first flight, she saw his distinctive dark head and tall figure below and quickened her steps. 'Mr Harman . . . !'

Hearing her voice, Ross paused and looked up in slight surprise. Phyllida waved the folder at him, unsmiling. He nodded and waited for her to reach him. Anxious to complete the errand and escape, she whisked around a corner and sped down the next flight—and missed her footing. She made a vain grab for the rail and bumped painfully down several of the stone steps, folder flying out of her hand and scattering his papers in all directions.

Ross bounded up the stairs at the first anguished cry and found her struggling to her feet, bruised and shaken.

'You really are too much, Phyllida!' he exclaimed, so relieved to find that she wasn't lying in a crumpled heap that it came out as exasperation.

Tears welled. Tears of pain from a rapidly swelling ankle and a badly bruised back and tears of humiliation that once again she had lived up to her reputation for being accident-prone.

'Oh, go to hell!' she snapped, fighting the tears and wishing it had been anyone but Ross who had come to her rescue.

It was so unexpected that he stared. Then he smiled down at her, in warm understanding. 'I'll have a look at that foot first,' he said firmly.

Gingerly, Phyllida tried her weight and winced. 'It's fine,' she said, although it obviously wasn't.

Ross made her sit down and ran expert hands over her foot and ankle. A little group had gathered, much to Phyllida's embarrassment. One or two offered advice.

'Is there a doctor in the house?' A passing wit raised a laugh and even Phyllida managed to smile.

'Do you hurt anywhere else?' Ross demanded.

'My back . . . a little. It's just bruised,' she said reluctantly, thinking it was quite time that he released her foot from his strong, capable hands with their almost caressing touch and wishing that she wasn't so aware of him as he crouched beside her on the stone stairs.

Someone had thoughtfully gathered up the wayward papers and restored them to the folder. 'Here you are, Nurse . . . '

'They're mine,' Ross said absently, taking the folder with a murmur of thanks. He smiled at Phyllida reassuringly. 'I'm sure it's just a bad sprain, but we'll have it X-rayed to be on the safe side.' Catching sight of a porter with an empty wheelchair on his way from one of the wards, he hailed him and within moments had commandeered the chair with his smiling charm and installed Phyllida in it and was heading for the X-ray Department despite her protests.

People stared, some amused, some merely intrigued

and others disbelieving, at the sight of a nurse in cap and apron being pushed along the corridors in a wheelchair by a doctor in his long white coat.

'I feel such an idiot!' Phyllida declared, face scarlet with embarrassment. 'And Sister will wonder what's happened to me!'

'I daresay she knows already,' Ross said, very dry. 'But I shall explain it all to her. Don't worry about a thing, Phyllida.' He put his hand to her soft, flushed face and left it there for a brief moment, knowing a protective kind of tenderness towards her that surprised and warmed his heart.

Phyllida stiffened at his touch and moved her head so that his hand fell away. It was easy for him, she thought resentfully. He could smile and speak and behave as though last night had never happened. It wasn't *his* pride that had been dragged in the dust or *his* heart that ached through rejection and the bitter conviction that loving would never bring any happiness in its wake.

It was easy for him to be kind, to show concern, although it contrasted oddly with the ruthless streak that enabled him to use and discard women with heartless sensuality. She didn't want his kindness or his sympathy or the warm friendliness that he was offering. If she couldn't have his love then she wanted nothing at all from him, she thought proudly.

X-rays showed that nothing was broken. She had sprained her ankle and bruised the small of her back and badly damaged her pride but she would be fit for work within a week.

Ross hurried off to Outpatients as soon as he had seen the X-ray plates that confirmed his diagnosis. Phyllida's ankle was strapped and she was sent back to the Nurses' Home to rest.

Feeling sore and shaken and rather sorry for herself, she settled on the shabby sofa with her books to study, determined to make some use of her enforced days off duty.

Less than half an hour later, there was a knock on the door of the little flat and she hobbled to open it.

Kevin, all concern after hearing of her accident through the hospital grapevine, had snatched some time from his very busy day to visit her. With a smile and a flourish, he produced a paper bag from behind his back.

'Grapes!' Phyllida couldn't help laughing. 'But I'm not ill!'

'A little spoiling never hurt anyone,' he said firmly. 'Get back on that sofa and I'll make you a cup of tea.'

'Does Sister Vernon know you're here?' she asked curiously. For Home Sister was very strict on the signing in of visitors and their departure before the stroke of midnight.

'Of course. She gave me her blessing. I think the old duck has a soft spot for you, Phyllida.' He put a cushion behind her back to make her more comfortable and dropped a light kiss on her curls. 'So have I, love . . . '

She caught at his hand, grateful for his niceness, wondering why she couldn't have chosen Kevin if she had been so ripe for falling in love.

'I suppose the entire place is buzzing? Trust me to fall down the stairs!'

'I gather that you landed at Ross Harman's feet. There must be easier ways to attract the man's attention,' he teased, busy with filling the kettle at the tiny sink.

She wrinkled her nose at him. 'Oh no! What's a sprained ankle and a bruised back?'

'I hear that he was very solicitous.'

She shrugged. 'He was very professional,' she amended, non-committal. 'On-the-spot diagnosis confirmed by immediate X-ray. Thank heavens it *is* only a sprain. I shall hate being away from the ward even for a few days when we're so busy.'

Kevin turned to look at her. 'You really enjoy nursing, don't you? I suppose you wouldn't give it up for anything—or anyone?'

Phyllida was instantly sensitive to a certain significance in the words. 'I'd like to finish my training, get my badge. That's what it's all about, isn't it? If I get married, I'll give up nursing to have children, of course. But I'd miss it and I'd want to go back to it as soon as I could,' she said lightly.

'I'm not thinking of getting married for a few years,' he said carefully. 'You'd have plenty of time to get your badge.'

Her heart gave an odd little jump as she realised that he was proposing to her in a roundabout way. 'Meaning . . . ?'

'Meaning I love you and I want to marry you, Phyllida.' He sat on the edge of the sofa, took her hand. 'We'd be a good team, love—and I'd do my best to make you happy.'

She rested her cheek on his shoulder. 'I don't love you, Kevin.' She had to be honest. Being Phyllida, she just couldn't be anything else.

'Not yet, I know.' He took it well. He raised her hand to his lips and pressed a kiss into the palm. 'But I'm working on that. Just give me a little more time,' he said cheerfully, smiling into her eyes.

Phyllida put an arm about his neck and kissed him, warmly affectionate. 'It might take a very long time . . .'

'I'll risk it.' He drew her into his arms, heartened that she had not given him an outright refusal. 'Couldn't we be engaged in the meantime?'

His embrace was light, reassuring, comforting because it demanded so little and offered so much. She leaned against him, liking him, warming to him, wishing with all her heart that she did love him. Kevin was so reliable and honest and good-hearted. He would not hurt her or let her down. He would not take her on a storm of passion and then bid her a cold and careless farewell. And it seemed that he really did love her.

She should say no and mean it. It was only fair when she knew that she would never love him and that her body couldn't respond to him as he wished.

'I'll think about it,' she said gently and kissed him . . .

CHAPTER TEN

PHYLLIDA was lonely, although Sister Vernon looked in on her occasionally and friends on varying shifts of duty drifted in and out for a gossip and to bring her the latest news from the hospital.

The loneliness was centred in the region of her heart. Kept busy on the ward, she might have had little time to fret, to remember over and over again every detail of that evening with Ross . . . the magic and the misery.

Lying on the divan bed in the rather cluttered living room with only her books for company, his handsome face was etched too vividly on her mind's eye and the echo of his voice was heard too clearly in her ear and the memory of his touch, his kiss, his urgent body against her own was a torment.

It was small comfort to know that he had gone out of his way to intercept Patti with an enquiry about Phyllida's injured ankle and sent his regards. Her friend had passed on the message with an amused and slightly suspicious twinkle in her eyes.

'Nice of him,' Phyllida had said as airily as she could, concealing a pang that he hadn't even sent her a friendly note. It was foolish to think that he might have found his way to the flat on the third floor of the Nurses' Home— or even wanted to see her. 'But it's the least he could do seeing that it was partly his fault! If he hadn't left those papers I wouldn't have had to dash after him and then I wouldn't have slipped on those wretched stairs!'

'He seemed very concerned about you.' If Patti thought it was unusual for a registrar to show an interest in a first-year, she did not say so . . . but she remembered that Phyllida had gone out with him one evening, surprising her friends who thought her much too level-headed to be swayed by the looks and the charm of one of Hartlake's busiest Casanovas. There was a ripple of rumour going about Hartlake that they had been seen together on other occasions, too. For such a friendly, open-hearted girl, Phyllida had been oddly reticent about the registrar. Patti was inclined to wonder if her friend waved the affair with Kevin Lawson as a camouflage for a much warmer interest in the other man.

'He was very kind at the time,' Phyllida conceded, rather grudgingly . . . and wished that Patti would stop talking about Ross when it hurt her so much even to think about him.

Sensitive to a certain note in her friend's voice, Patti dropped the subject and very soon was hurrying back to Hartlake for the rest of the day's work, having snatched a few precious minutes out of her lunch break to hurry to the Nurses' Home and see if there was anything she could do for Phyllida. She was a thoughtful and caring girl. It had been her idea to push the divan bed to the window so that Phyllida might see what was going on while she rested the still-swollen and rather painful ankle.

The window overlooked the High Street with its steady stream of cars and buses and lorries, the popular street market with its array of stalls and the row of shops opposite the main entrance to the hospital. Phyllida could just see the pillared portico and the wide stone steps if she craned her neck. But the sight of doctors and nurses and patients making their way in and out of Hartlake only made her feel more keenly the stupidity of the accident that had left Paterson short-staffed that week.

She sighed and reached for a textbook on Surgical Nursing. But that only reminded her of Ross, who had probably spent much of his day in Theatres, busy with the business of saving lives while she fretted at her enforced idleness.

She glanced at her watch. Kate would be off-duty at four and it would be nice to have a pot of tea ready for her return. Perhaps if she kept most of her weight on the good foot, she could manage. She swung her feet to the floor and hobbled painfully to the small sink to fill the kettle and switch it on to boil.

'Feeling better, Phyll . . . ?' One of her set, hurrying past the open door with a clean apron over her arm, saw her and called a friendly enquiry, but didn't pause for an answer.

Phyllida set out cups and found a packet of biscuits. She opened a cupboard to take out the big box of tea-bags, reached up for it.

'Why aren't you resting that ankle?'

The deep voice startled her so much that she dropped the economy-size box—and stood in the midst of a sea of tea-bags, staring at him defensively. 'I am!'

He shook his head at her, the familiar glow of amusement coupled with a hint of warm tenderness lurking in his eyes and his smile. She had coloured up, the blush leaping into her small face and staining the slender throat and even tinging the lovely swell of her breast, slightly exposed by the fall of the kaftan-style cotton robe that she was wearing. It was a very hot day. He knew with a sudden stir of his senses that she had nothing on beneath the gown.

Phyllida felt the heat in her face and the quick, tingling excitement running through her for the mere sight of him, so attractive and so endearing with that smile in his dark eyes. She was puzzled and pleased and a little dismayed to see him. It was very likely that he had simply walked into the Nurses' Home and made his way up to the third floor without so much as a word to Home Sister or anyone else. And Nancy's light words as she dashed past the open door had obviously identified the flat she shared with her friends at just the right moment.

He came into the room and closed the door. Her eyes widened. 'What are you doing!' she exclaimed, horrified. 'Leave the door open or you'll have Sister Vernon visualising all manner of wickedness!'

He laughed. 'She could be right!' He moved towards her. She stiffened, backed away slightly. Ross raised an eyebrow. 'You look like a startled fawn. Surely I don't frighten you, Phyllida,' he protested lightly.

'Sister Vernon frightens me,' she said firmly, with truth. Entertaining friends in the flat was one thing. Entertaining a senior doctor with *his* reputation behind closed doors would certainly arouse suspicions and might mean the threat of dismissal.

'Sister Vernon and I are old friends,' he told her reassuringly.

'Oh, of course! Stupid of me not to realise it. I expect you worked your way through *her* set, too—in your medical student days!' She was tart because she was very much on the defensive.

'Before my time!' He was amused. 'Do I look so old, for heaven's sake? I'm only twenty-eight!'

'It must be the life you lead!'

He grinned appreciatively. 'Get off that ankle and don't talk so much. Show a little respect for my grey hairs!' He stooped to scoop up a handful of the scattered tea-bags from the floor. 'I want you fit for Founder's Ball.'

Phyllida found herself crouching to help, his dark head very near to her own, her heart pounding like a wild thing. She wanted to put her arms about him in warm welcome. She wanted to cry. She wanted to send him away and tell him never to see her again because she couldn't bear him to be nice when there was no future in it. 'I'm not going to Founder's Ball,' she said coolly.

He smiled. 'Not even with me?'

It was the big event of the hospital year when everyone let their hair down and thoroughly enjoyed themselves. For one night of the year, even Matron relaxed and smiled on flirtatious nurses and amorous young doctors who made the most of their opportunities. Many a romance had apparently begun with an exchange of glances at Founder's Ball.

It was an unwritten Hartlake maxim that if a doctor or medical student invited a nurse to go with him to Founder's Ball then he was thinking seriously of becoming permanently involved in some way. So Phyllida was startled by that smiling invitation and baffled that he should ask her when he had been so adamant that their all-too-brief relationship must end.

How could a girl ever know where she was with a man like Ross?

She closed the lid of the box firmly on the last of the rescued tea-bags, straightened up. 'No.' It cost her something to deny herself the delight of dancing in his arms and the satisfaction of being seen by others as important to him . . . particularly Georgy Knight! But she thought of Kevin who loved her and to whom she owed a degree of loyalty because she had half-promised to marry him one day. She didn't owe Ross anything but heartache and humiliation and she didn't mean to invite any more of the same, she told herself firmly.

She put her weight unwarily on the injured foot and ouched involuntarily, put out a hand for support and clutched unthinkingly at his arm, promptly at her service.

'Is it still so painful?' he asked gently, concerned.

'It isn't too bad. I just stepped badly. The worst part is the boredom of doing nothing,' she admitted wryly.

'Then why not go home until you're fit to return to duty?' he suggested. 'I'll take you, Phyllida. My car is at your disposal and I'm off duty tomorrow. I'll bring you back when you're ready, too. Just call me.'

She looked at him, surprised and doubtful. She was tempted to take him up on the offer. But hadn't she resolved to keep him out of her life as much as possible?

'That's very kind . . .' Phyllida began in careful preliminary to polite refusal.

Ross smiled down at her warmly. 'No, it isn't. I've an ulterior motive, of course. How could you doubt it?' Amusement flickered as he saw the sudden wariness cross the small face. 'I'll take you to your home and bring you back again—and in return you come with me to the Ball. Fair enough?'

Her momentary tension relaxed, ebbed away. She nodded. 'All right . . . '

She longed to be at home with her family for a few days, cosseted by her mother and comforted by the close relationship that she shared with her father. Home seemed to offer the only real security where love and trust could always be relied on. She would use Ross to go home, impossible by public transport until her ankle was very much better—and take a chance on having to keep her part of the bargain and hurt Kevin. He might easily have changed his mind about taking her when the time came. Founder's Ball was more than a fortnight away and someone else would probably attract his fickle attention in the meantime.

Phyllida abruptly abandoned the idea of making tea. Her ankle was aching and her back was hurting and she knew that she had been on her feet long enough. 'You're right. I should be resting my ankle,' she said ruefully. 'I'd better sit down . . . '

Ross put an arm about her waist and swung her effortlessly up and carried her across to the narrow bed with its piled cushions that turned it into a couch by day. Phyllida bit her lip to keep back the instinctive protest and made the most of the unexpected contact with him . . . like any fool in love, she thought wryly.

He laid her gently against the cushions, his arms lingering about her because they had ached so much to hold her over the last few days.

Her body stirred at the look in his eyes, reminding her of magic moments. She resisted the temptation and the

need to slide her arms about his neck and lift her face to
be kissed.

'Let me go, Ross,' she said quietly, trying hard to be
resolute and level-headed.

He smiled into her eyes. 'I want you,' he said, slow
and quiet, as if the words were forced to the surface from
the depths of him by the strength of his feelings, against
his will. And so they were. For a man like Ross found it
hard to admit that there was one woman in the world
who threatened to tame his wild sensuality and keep him
captive for the rest of his life. 'I want you very much . . .'
he murmured, soft and convincing. He kissed her, hard
and urgent, quickening to fierce and thrusting desire as
her warm mouth was surprised into sweet and tremulous
response.

Phyllida knew that her body leaped with answering
desire. She thrust him away but it was too late for him
not to know it, too. She saw the glint of male triumph in
the dark eyes and sighed with regret for her weakness.
He curved his strong hand about her breast with the
confidence of the lover who already knew her body too
intimately. She quickly covered it with her own, meaning to check the caress that made her melt and then she
was suddenly too weak with wanting to stop him from
making sensuous love to her. She sighed again . . . a sigh
of surrender as the tremulous shiver of desire ran
through her slight body and she gave herself up to the
potency of his kiss, his touch, the ardour of his body
suddenly heavy on her own.

Their lips met eagerly and the flame burned fierce and
his skilled hands on her sensitive body beneath the thin
cotton robe roused her to a torment of longing that only

his urgent and demanding sexuality could ease.

Wanting her was a fever in his blood that would not be denied. He took her with only the satisfaction of his senses in mind but he discovered a sexual delight such as he had never found in any other woman's arms. It was not only the eager and incredibly exciting response of a girl who had only just realised her own sensuality. There was so much more to making love to Phyllida. He experienced a new tenderness and a selfless concern for her fulfilment and there was a kind of glory in the shared and tumultuous climax of passion.

Phyllida clung to him, shaken and shocked by that readiness to let him make love to her without a thought for anything but the magic of the moment. It had been sudden and spontaneous wanting between a man and a woman who fired each other at a glance, a touch, to very dangerous flame.

Her body melted in his arms, glowing in the golden aftermath of lovemaking, and her heart throbbed with love and longing for him. But the level head would not be silenced any longer and it insisted that she was all kinds of a fool to lie in his embrace and be so gloriously loved when it meant so little to him—and when there was every risk that Kate would walk in or that Sister Vernon would make another of her sporadic checks on a nurse on sick leave.

Reluctantly, she stirred. 'Ross . . . ?' She touched her hand to the dark curls of the head that was heavy on her bare breast.

He raised his head, smiled into her eyes. Then he touched his lips to her own. 'Phyllida,' he said softly, taking her name and turning it into an endearment.

She was learning the ways of love, she thought with a suddenly heavy heart. Love as he knew it, anyway. Now, he said her name like a lover, spent and content in her arms. But in an hour, she would be forgotten, unimportant—until the next time that his body was on fire for her. It wasn't love at all. She was not that much of a fool. Just fool enough to love him too much to have denied him that ecstatic communion—or herself, she admitted with rueful candour.

'There'll be hell to pay if Sister finds you here . . . like this,' she said, sighing. 'You'll get away with it, of course. I won't!'

He rolled away from her. 'True . . .' He smiled wryly. 'I don't usually behave so irresponsibly. What is it about you that makes a man so reckless?'

'My body?' she suggested, very dry.

His eyes narrowed. 'Not just your body,' he said, very firm.

She didn't believe him. 'It must be my beautiful face—or my bank balance,' she said, lightly teasing.

'I don't know about your bank balance,' he returned, equally light. 'But I love your beautiful face.' He drew her to him and covered her startled and very sweet face with kisses . . . her forehead, her eyes, her small and shapely nose, her flushed cheeks and the stubborn little chin. His lips lingered at her mouth.

Phyllida's foolish heart soared at the warm tenderness in those butterfly kisses, very ready to interpret the look in his eyes as loving. Her level head dragged it firmly back to earth with the stern reminder that he was a sensual and utterly heartless rake who was never likely to love her or any other girl for real.

He was a very dangerous man. She had lost her heart and her virginity to him in a very short space of time. If she continued to fall into his arms every time he decided to want her, she would soon lose her self-respect, too. She knew she ought to end the affair that was not really an affair at all—before he did and with finality the next time!

But perhaps she could allow herself to store up just a few more golden memories for the future, she thought wistfully. For she loved him so much and she had so little to remember . . .

He left her with a promise to come for her in his car the following morning. Phyllida was torn between a longing to spend as much time as possible with him while she could and a reluctance to drive with him into Essex. It would mean introducing him to her family and that would lead to all kinds of questions to which she didn't have the answers. Her parents were loving and concerned and she had always been so open about her affairs. But there had never been anyone in her life quite like Ross and she didn't know how to explain him!

Kate passed the good-looking registrar on the stairs and looked after him, intrigued. Then she hurried on to the flat, curious to know what had brought him to the Nurses' Home and wondering if Phyllida had achieved the almost-miracle of capturing more than Ross Harman's fleeting interest.

'You're late,' Phyllida greeted her lightly, trying not to sound too thankful for it and trying not to look as if she had just risen from a lover's ardent embrace.

'Shopping.' Kate dumped a carrier bag on the table and began to unload it. 'I've just seen Ross Harman on his way down. Taking a professional interest in a very rare case of sprained ankle-itis, is he?' she teased gently, affectionate laughter lurking in her eyes.

A little colour sprang into Phyllida's face but she smiled. 'He called in to see me,' she admitted, rather reluctantly, but knowing that it must be obvious that he had been in the flat. It had been such a close-run thing that he and Kate must have passed on the stairs. Phyllida dreaded to think how everyone would have felt if Kate had been only ten minutes earlier! 'He seems to feel that he's responsible for my fall,' she added, trying to offer some kind of explanation for his interest that her friend would accept without question.

Kate chuckled. 'Oh . . . ?' The laughing murmur was pregnant with unmistakable meaning.

Now, Phyllida's face flamed as she realised her unfortunate choice of words. 'On the stairs!' she said firmly, throwing a cushion at her friend in light-hearted reproach. Kate caught it deftly. 'Don't leap to conclusions!'

'Even if they are the right ones,' Kate said, smiling. 'I don't know that I blame you if you have fallen for him. He *is* a charmer. But I thought he was so involved with that staff nurse on Paterson? There's been a lot of gossip about them going away together.'

'So he is.' Phyllida carefully kept all the dislike and jealousy of that involvement out of her light tone. 'He's just being friendly.'

'Never trust a man who offers to be your friend,' Kate warned blithely. 'It's much more dangerous than blatant pursuit!'

'You don't need to warn me about a man like Ross

Harman. I'm not quite a fool,' Phyllida declared, thinking how much she would hate her friend to know that the warning was much too late.

'Even if you do like him!' Kate smiled at her warmly. 'By the way, I've a message for you from Kevin. He's managed to get someone to take over his duty hours this evening and he's coming round about eight o'clock. Popular girl, aren't you?'

Phyllida felt a twinge of guilt at the mention of Kevin. In all fairness, she ought to tell him that her affection for him would never turn into love and that she had been very wrong to encourage him in the hope that they might marry one day.

She was a little afraid of the wanton desire that Ross stirred so easily, making her forget Kevin and every other consideration in the need for that wonderful world of delight in his strong arms. But at least it was born of loving. So she knew just why Kevin's kiss, Kevin's touch, Kevin's arms about her made her warm to him without the slightest breath of passion in her response.

A man could enjoy lovemaking without wanting to love or to be loved. There were girls who felt the same way, too, encouraging and inviting sex without emotional involvement. Phyllida wasn't one of them. Her heart had to be inolved before she could give her body. For all the potency of his sexual attractions, she knew that she couldn't have lain in his arms if she didn't love Ross with a real and lasting love.

So it was not possible for her to think of marrying Kevin. He deserved so much more than the lukewarm affection that was all she could give him. She knew with a little sadness for Kevin and perhaps even more for herself that she would never be free of the love and the aching need that Ross had quickened in her, body and soul. But Phyllida knew that he wasn't ready to love any woman just yet—and least of all someone like herself.

She wasn't the first girl to love him and lose him. She wouldn't be the last . . .

CHAPTER ELEVEN

THE car consumed the miles rather too rapidly for Phyllida and she wondered if he was anxious to reach her home and drop her off and get back to town as soon as possible. Maybe he was meeting Georgy later in the day—or some other girl. Any woman in Ross Harman's life had to accept the fact that she was far from being the only one, she thought wryly.

He had called for her at the Nurses' Home promptly on time, helped her down to his car with a solicitous arm about her waist, settled her comfortably beside him and set off on the forty-mile journey—giving up his valuable time for her sake. How could she help liking as well as loving him? It would be so much easier to stop caring and forget all about him if he wasn't so nice, she felt.

As he drove, she admired his skilful handling of the fast car and was very relaxed by his side despite the amount of traffic on the main arterial road into the heart of Essex. But he seemed to be good at everything. He was a darling of the gods with his looks and charm and intelligence, the wealthy background and expensive education, the surgical ability that had gained him the much-envied post as the Professor's registrar and the probability that he would become a consultant at an unusually early age. He was one of Hartlake's most eligible bachelors and so many girls ran after him that it wouldn't be surprising if he was thoroughly spoiled.

148

Phyllida didn't think that he was, in fact.

She had found him kind and caring and very tender and the woman that he eventually loved with all his heart would be very, very lucky. She sighed.

Ross turned his head to smile. 'Sad to be leaving all those bedpans behind for a few days?' he asked, eyes twinkling. 'Or is that sigh for the thought of not seeing me?'

'I mean to forget about bedpans and books and everything connected with Hartlake—including you,' she said firmly.

Ross put a hand lightly on her knee. 'Don't forget about me completely. We have a date.'

Phyllida felt a tremor run through her at the warmth of his hand through the thin material of her dress. 'I suppose you mean the Ball?'

'Of course.'

'My ankle may not be strong enough for dancing by then,' she warned.

'Then we'll sit and talk all evening. Don't renege on me, Phyllida. We made a bargain.'

She smiled slightly. 'Georgy might have other plans for you.'

'No one makes plans for me . . . *ever*!'

She saw the glint of anger in the dark eyes and wondered wryly if any woman would ever humble that proud independence.

'You might meet some other girl and regret our bargain,' she said lightly, feeling that it was only too likely.

'If I do, I'll tell you so.' He was a trifle curt. 'But I don't expect to be looking for other girls.' Abruptly, he pulled off the road into a convenient lay-by and parked, switched off the engine. Then he turned to look at her with a slight frown in his eyes. '*You* are regretting it. That's what you mean, isn't it?'

'I hope you won't dump me in this lay-by if I say yes,' she said, trying to keep it light.

'I might be tempted!'

She smiled at him. 'You aren't the type.'

He raised an eyebrow, faintly amused. 'Oh, yes, I am!'

'You just like to play the part of the villain.' Needing to touch him, moved by loving, she laid her hand along his lean cheek, a slightly tremulous smile hovering about her mouth. 'You have a great deal of heart, I think.'

He turned his head slightly to kiss the slender fingers. Then he trapped them in his own and leaned to kiss her lips. She responded with swift, sweet warmth and he was suddenly swept with aching desire.

'Must you go home?' he asked abruptly. 'Why don't we drive to the coast, book into a hotel for the night? I'm off duty for two days.'

She shook her head, regretful. 'My parents are expecting me.'

'Telephone them!' he urged, warm and coaxing. 'I'll take you there tomorrow. Give me tonight.' He put an arm about her and nuzzled her soft neck with warm, sensual lips. 'Please, Phyllida . . .' He was tense, throbbing with the passion she evoked so strongly in him.

She couldn't explain her reluctance when her body leaped with excitement at the mere thought of spending a night in his arms. But she knew it was to do with spontaneity and cold blood. She could melt when he

held her, kissed her, without warning and find it impossible to deny him anything. But when it came to a dispassionate proposal and the necessary planning for a night
with him in a hotel bedroom, she felt that it cheapened
their relationship.

'I can't do that,' she said firmly. But she cradled his
dark head with a tender hand to soften the blow of the
refusal.

Ross sighed, straightened up and turned his head to
look at the constant stream of traffic that passed their
parked car. He thought with longing of making love to
her and then sleeping with his arms about her and
waking to a new day to find her there, beside him, bright
hair on the pillow, lips and arms and lovely body ready to
receive him again. He was beginning to feel that he
wanted her with him for always. He didn't understand
her reluctance, her refusal. He didn't like it. A little
anger began to simmer because he was not used to
pleading for what he wanted. He had never had to plead.
Proud, independent and spoiled by his success with
women, it irritated him that instead of eager delight at
his suggestion she had coolly turned him down.

Phyllida regarded him unhappily, sensing the anger
that was born of frustration, sorry to disappoint him but
feeling that he should not expect too much of her even if
he did know that she loved him.

Fighting her own disappointment, she said carefully:
'There isn't any future in it, Ross.'

She was trying to say without reproach that she knew
and accepted that she was only a temporary interest in
his life. It wasn't his fault that she had fallen in love
without the least encouragement, after all.

She was trying to say that, although she did not regret anything that had happened between them, she didn't want to build up too much heartache for herself by letting it go on.

His eyes narrowed abruptly. 'Does there have to be a future? Can't we just enjoy what we have going for each other right now?' Dismayed that she was just like all the others, trying to pin him down, stooping to a kind of blackmail to extort promises of lasting commitment before graciously giving her body, he was suddenly angry. 'Women are all the same,' he said, bitter in disappointment. 'You're supposed to be sentimental and generous creatures of impulse. In my experience, you're all as hard as nails and determined to drag a man to the altar by hook or by crook!'

Phyllida was shocked and bruised by the angry words and instantly inflamed by their injustice. For when had she ever asked anything of him or implied that she wanted to marry him?

'Don't flatter yourself!' she flared hotly. 'I wouldn't marry you if you were the last man on earth! I didn't make myself clear, obviously. I was trying to say that I'm going to marry Kevin Lawson. That's why I won't spend the night with you—and why I've no intention of going to Founder's Ball with you!'

He looked at her steadily, searching the very blue eyes. She looked back at him with defiant pride. 'Then why isn't Lawson driving you home instead of me?' he asked, very dry.

Her chin tilted. 'He's on duty and you're not. He can't afford the petrol and you can. You offered—and I'd have been a fool to refuse!'

A little amusement flickered in his eyes. He shook his head. 'Sorry. It's a brave try but I don't believe that you're just using me—or that you're engaged to Lawson.'

Phyllida shrugged. 'Please yourself.' She glanced pointedly at her watch. 'Can we get on, do you think? My mother is expecting us for lunch.'

Ross chuckled. 'You're putting a lot of faith in my goodness of heart, aren't you? After that outburst, I ought to make you walk—or hitch a lift! But I suppose I asked for it. I'm not a very good loser, I'm afraid.' He smiled at her, very warm.

She recognised the melting of his mood as a near-apology but she didn't think that she was ready to forgive him. 'You aren't used to losing!' she said tartly.

'That's true. And I'm not going to lose you, Phyllida. Not to Lawson or anyone else,' he returned, swift and sure.

She bridled slightly at the confidence of the words and manner. 'I'm not yours to lose!'

He smiled at the show of spirit. Then he leaned towards her and kissed her lightly, a warm glow in his dark eyes. 'You're mine for as long as I want you,' he said softly, against the cool, unforgiving lips. 'And I want you very much . . .'

How could any woman resist the flattering warmth of his tone, the way he smiled and looked and kissed her? Phyllida was a woman in love and lost in the magic of his kiss, her lips warming and parting, her arm sliding about his neck on a sigh.

She wondered how she was going to get through the long and lonely days before she saw him again. Her heart wrenched in sudden despair that it should be her destiny to fall so deeply in love with a man like Ross . . .

Her parents took an instant liking to him. Phyllida had wondered if a too-attractive and obviously worldly stranger, some years older than herself, would arouse suspicion in a protective mother and a loving father. But they did not seem to recognise him as a rake who was a danger to their daughter. She knew the potency of his charm but she was still surprised as well as pleased by the friendly and welcoming reception that her parents gave him.

Drusilla was more aware. She was young enough to be impressed by looks and charm but she had good reason to be on her guard against his kind. 'Known him long?' she asked quietly while Phyllida cuddled up her small niece and Ross talked to their father.

'A few weeks.'

'Watch your step,' Drusilla warned, knowing all the pitfalls and anxious that her elder sister should not make her mistake. 'He looks dangerous.'

Phyllida smiled. 'We're just friends,' she said lightly.

Drusilla caught the slight hint of defence in eyes and voice. 'Yes, I know,' she said gently, warm understanding behind the words. 'But he's the love 'em and leave 'em type, isn't he? You will be careful, won't you?'

Phyllida chose not to answer. She buried her face in the moist, sweet-smelling warmth of Amy's chubby neck and the baby gurgled with delight. She was a pretty child with dark blue eyes and bright chestnut curls like her own.

Ross glanced across and thought how pretty Phyllida looked, laughing with her small niece, and for no reason at all his heart suddenly turned over in his breast. He was shaken, dismayed. Loving made too many demands on a man. He wasn't ready for loving. The way he felt about her couldn't possibly have turned into loving without him knowing—or could it?

After an excellent lunch during which he had plenty of opportunity to observe that they were a close and affectionate family, her parents tactfully withdrew to wash the dishes and Amy was whisked off to her afternoon nap by Drusilla.

Phyllida smiled at him. 'I hope you aren't feeling overwhelmed.' She was slightly embarrassed, hoping he didn't suppose that she had given her parents the wrong impression about their relationship.

'Not at all.' Ross turned from the window where he had been contemplating the small but very well-kept garden. He sat down beside her on the sofa and stretched his long legs, replete and relaxed and oddly reluctant to start the drive back to London. 'It's nice to feel so welcome—and your mother is a superb cook. One day I'll get to find out if you can do as well, I hope.'

'I didn't think you were interested in my culinary talents,' she said, teasing him, eyes bright with the happiness she found in his company. She had never expected to see him beneath her parents' roof, so much at home and slipping into easy intimacy with her family as though he had known them for ever, and it was heart-warming.

'I'm interested in everything about you,' he returned promptly. He slid an arm about her and drew her towards him and she smiled into his dark eyes and kissed him lightly, with love. It was so natural, so open, that it touched his heart. His arm tightened. 'I said that I didn't mean to get involved,' he said, rueful. 'But you seem to have bewitched me. I like you too much. I like being with you too much. I like making love to you too much.' He put his hand to her cheek in a caress. Then he trailed his fingers lightly down the slender throat to the curve of her breast in a lover's touch. 'I shall miss you . . .'

She quivered at his touch on her vulnerable body. Her heart lurched at the look in his eyes, that meaningful murmur.

'You won't have time to miss me,' she said, lightly, because she knew he would draw back from any hint of intensity. 'I'll be back at Hartlake in a few days.'

'Don't forget that I'm driving you back. Ring me when you're ready . . . and maybe we'll get that night together, after all,' he added, soft, very persuasive. 'Even if I have to run out of petrol on the way back to town!'

Phyllida laughed. 'I shall be quite capable of taking a train. I'm a fraud, anyway. My ankle was much better this morning.'

'Ring me!' he said, firm.

She gave him a quick, affectionate hug. 'Don't be so nice to me!' she exclaimed, laughing, although her heart ached because, deep down inside, she knew that the future held certain disappointment for all the promise of his interest and attention. 'I won't want to part with you when you fall for some other girl!'

Ross smiled, kissed her. But he didn't tell her that it would never happen. He knew himself too well. She was delightful, enchanting, very sweet—and she did things to his heart that he had never known before. But he was reluctant to call it loving. That would be a very final commitment, he felt.

He was glad that she didn't trust him or expect too much of him. He was glad that she was such a level-headed and sensitive girl, fond of him and obviously attracted to him but far from being in love as he had once feared. It wouldn't break her heart when he turned to someone else with the swift sexual wanting that seemed to thrust aside every other consideration. He was glad that he wasn't the only man in Phyllida's life and that she had someone like Kevin Lawson to console her when the fierce flame of their mutual passion eventually burned itself out.

But Ross discovered that he wasn't glad at all when Georgy told him that the engagement he had dismissed as proud pretence was very much a reality. It seemed that everyone at Hartlake but himself knew that Phyllida was going to marry Kevin Lawson. The houseman had spread the news among his friends even if she had meant him to keep it secret for the time being.

Ross continued to write up an antibiotic drug on a patient's chart with an admirably steady hand. But he was seeing Phyllida's small, sweet face and those candid blue eyes very vividly against the white page and wondering with sick dismay why she had lain in his arms and let him grow to love her when she meant to marry another man. He had thought her so honest, so straight—and she had turned out to be a cheat like every woman he had ever known.

'Grapevine gossip,' he said dismissively.

Georgy scanned the handsome, dispassionate face. 'Yes, that's what I thought,' she agreed. 'But Kevin

Lawson told me himself only yesterday. She's a flirtatious girl and I didn't take much notice of the snatched moments on the ward. You know what the juniors are like with anything in a white coat. Even registrars aren't always safe,' she added lightly, cleverly. 'But it seems that it was serious, after all. They really are engaged.'

He returned the chart to the rail at the foot of the bed and glanced at the patient who was still sleeping off the effects of anaesthetic.

Seventeen years old and living by herself in a bedsit in one of the shabby streets that bordered the hospital, she had been brought in as an emergency in the early hours of the morning. As duty registrar, Ross had been called from his bed to perform the appendicectomy. It had been an abrupt and familiar ending to his brief spell of leave, some of it spent with Phyllida and the rest of it in thinking about her and longing for her. Now, he thought grimly that there was no fool like a man who allowed himself to fall in love against his better judgment—and with a girl who was no different from any other, after all.

'Good luck to them,' he said carelessly, turning away and beginning to walk briskly towards the ward doors. 'I can't say that I'm particularly interested in Lawson's affairs. I really don't know the man very well.'

Georgy had fallen into step by his side, outwardly the efficient staff nurse in charge of the ward while Sister enjoyed a much-deserved coffee break, simmering inside with a kind of anger. His indifferent tone and manner were reassuring. Somehow, she wasn't reassured.

She wasn't in love with Ross but that didn't prevent her from being jealous of his other women. She had been suspicious of his obvious liking for Phyllida Sims for some time. She had forgiven but she hadn't forgotten the way he had answered the telephone at his flat one evening, like a man interrupted in lovemaking and annoyed about it—and Georgy wouldn't be surprised to learn that the first-year had been in bed with him. He had made a great deal of unnecessary fuss over a sprained ankle, too, apparently. It was not really surprising that there had been a ripple of rumour about a registrar's interest in a very junior nurse.

'No, perhaps not,' she agreed lightly, smiling. 'But I think you've a soft spot for the girl. People have been talking and sometimes there's more than a grain of truth in grapevine gossip. I suspect that you know each other better off the ward than on it, Ross.' Her tone was amused but it held a challenge.

He shrugged. 'People always talk. She's a pretty girl and I've paid her some attention. But she's as unreliable as all women.'

'Meaning that you got what you wanted when you least expected it—or didn't get it at all?'

She made the mistake of too many women of not being able to leave well alone, he thought with impatience. It must be obvious that he didn't want to discuss Phyllida. Equally obvious that he was determined to cut her out of his life, love her or not.

'For God's sake, Georgy! I don't make a habit of seducing first-years! Green girls are not my style,' he said with a harsh laugh.

'But you seduced Phyllida Sims.' It sounded like light-hearted, slightly amused acceptance of his incorrigible sensuality. But the expression in her eyes boded ill for an unsuspecting junior when she returned to Paterson from sick leave.

Ross had every intention of denying it. But before he could speak, Kevin Lawson came out of the side ward where he had been setting up an intravenous drip for a pre-operative patient and nodded so curtly to the registrar as he brushed past him that it was only too obvious that he had heard the exchange.

Ross looked after the man, eyes narrowed.

'Damn you, Georgy,' he said slowly, angry.

For the first time in his life, he knew what it meant to love—and to regret the careless way of life that had led to the taking of a girl who belonged to another man. Not necessarily because she loved him. Ross found it hard to accept that she did. But because she had obviously agreed to marry the man, for whatever reason. Knowing how he would feel if he stood in Lawson's shoes and had overheard a casual and contemptuous discussion of his fiancée's morals and behaviour, he sympathised with the houseman.

Georgy's chin went up swiftly. 'Damn *you*, Ross Harman!' she exclaimed, fierce and bitter in the sudden realisation that she had lost him completely. 'I hope you really care for her—and I hope it hurts!' She swept away down the ward, starched skirts crackling as though they expressed her fury.

Ross was due in Theatres and it was essential that he should be completely in control of his shaken emotions before he scrubbed up and donned mask and gown for the thoracoplasty that was the first operation on a long list.

Outside the ward, he stood for a few moments by one

of the long corridor windows, staring down at the hospital garden with its scurrying figures criss-crossing the paved paths, hands thrust deep into the pockets of his white coat and eyes dark with a pain that he had never expected to know.

Loving Phyllida, he didn't want to believe that she was a wanton and a cheat. But, engaged to another man, she had allowed him to take her to bed and responded with such eager sensuality to his embrace that if he hadn't known her to be virgin he would have supposed her very experienced in sexual delight.

Loving Phyllida, he didn't want to believe that she was a liar. But hadn't she lied with every smile, every glance, every word she had ever spoken and every kiss they had ever exchanged?

Loving Phyllida was a trap into which he had fallen all unawares. But at least no one knew it but himself . . .

CHAPTER TWELVE

PHYLLIDA pinned on her apron with slightly trembling fingers and checked that her cap was firmly in place on her rebellious curls. Eyes dark with excitement in a small, slightly flushed face looked back at her from the mirror in the junior's room. She couldn't be sure of seeing Ross that morning until she knew if any of Professor Wilson's patients were on Paterson. But she could hope—and she had missed him so much that every day away from Hartlake had seemed an eternity.

She had made her own way from her home in Essex, after all. She had telephoned the number he had given but she must have taken it down wrong. For it couldn't have been Ross who answered the telephone although it had sounded like his voice until she said, a little breathlessly: 'Ross? It's me—Phyllida.'

'You seem to have the wrong number,' the man had returned, surprisingly curt, and hung up.

Ross would never have spoken to her in that way—and why should he? His parting kiss had been particularly tender, his last words to her so warmly affectionate that her foolish heart had leaped with new hope.

Realising that she didn't have his address, she couldn't check the operator and there was no way she could reach him at the hospital. Very disappointed and hoping that he would believe that she had tried to get in touch with him, Phyllida had taken the train.

162

She had arrived back at Hartlake and the Nurses' Home to learn from her friends that she was engaged to Kevin. At first, she thought it just a joke. When they had convinced her that everyone was talking about the engagement, she had been more amused than angry with Kevin.

It was her fault for being so chicken and failing to make it clear to him that she was never likely to marry him, she knew. She was much too soft-hearted, far too fond of him and she had felt that the whole thing would eventually fizzle out if their relationship just drifted.

She didn't understand how he had managed to convey the impression that they were actually engaged. But rumours were thick on the ground at Hartlake and could arise out of the most casual remark. No doubt Kevin had merely mentioned to a friend that he hoped to marry her when she had completed her training and it had then been exaggerated out of all proportion.

Perhaps it hadn't seemed necessary to him to correct a false impression. After all, he was an optimist in love and she had encouraged him, rather foolishly, to think that she might marry him one day.

He didn't like her association with Ross, although she had stressed that it was a very ordinary friendship rather than admit that she had fallen in love with the registrar. He hadn't liked it when she told him that Ross was driving her into Essex, but he had accepted her assurance that there was nothing in their relationship to worry him. She must have been a little too convincing, she thought wryly, and made up her mind to break it gently to Kevin that they could never be anything but good friends.

She hoped that Ross didn't know what people were saying about her and Kevin. But her affairs couldn't be of very much interest to most people at Hartlake, she thought confidently. She had no way of knowing that Kevin had deliberately fostered the rumour with the intention that Ross Harman should learn of her commitment to another man and cool his attentions.

She had hurried to the ward for her first day's work since that fall on the stairs. She hoped to see Ross but it depended on whether he had occasion to visit Paterson. He probably didn't know that she was back, of course. She might have left a note for him with Jimmy at the desk in Main Hall. But she didn't want to seem too eager even if Ross knew that she loved him. And Phyllida didn't doubt that he knew for she must have betrayed it in so many ways . . .

Sister Hamilton observed the sparkle in the deep blue eyes, the hint of excited colour in the girl's face, recognising the symptoms with a little amusement. Love seemed to be the one disease that no amount of medical skill or science could prevent or cure, she thought dryly . . . and sometimes she felt that it was an occupational hazard in their profession! The cynics declared that marriage was the only cure and it was a pity that they so often seemed to be proved right. But she didn't mean to dash the happiness from the first-year's face by saying so. In fact, she didn't mean to mention the girl's engagement. There was no place for private matters on a busy ward and apparently it had not been officially announced.

Kevin Lawson was a nice young man and a capable doctor. Phyllida was a lucky girl and it wasn't at all surprising that her mind had been seldom on her work in recent weeks or that she had lost her footing on the stairs because her head had been in the clouds! Now that her future was more certain, perhaps she would settle down and fulfil her promise of being a very good nurse.

'I hope that ankle is really back to normal, Nurse Sims. You'll be run off your feet in the next few days,' she warned, a smile belying the brisk tone. 'Nurse Bell has scalded her hand and Nurse Wilmot is in Sick Bay with tonsillitis. So I'm very glad to have you back and I hope you'll keep your disasters to a minimum if only until I have my full quota of nurses again!'

Warming to the twinkle in her senior's eyes, Phyllida smiled back, quite radiant. 'Yes, Sister.'

'We're overdue with pulse and temps so you can start on that and then help with the washings.'

'Yes, Sister . . .'

The ward was full of unfamiliar names and faces. In the days that she had been away, patients had been discharged or transferred to other wards for more specialised care. One or two had died. Surgical wards gave a nurse little time to get to know patients, she had discovered. Mrs Schwodler had been an exception.

Most were admitted, operated on and then discharged within a matter of days, thanks to modern drugs and modern attitudes to surgery. Sometimes a patient felt that she was discharged too soon, sent home complete with sutures that would be taken out by a community nurse from the local health centre. But most patients couldn't wait to go home, grateful though they were for all that was done for them by the hard-working doctors and nurses at the famous teaching hospital that was held in such affection and respect.

Georgy Knight greeted her without warmth. 'So you're back to shatter the smooth running of the ward? Paterson just hasn't been the same without you!'

Phyllida smiled, refusing to take offence at the venom behind the words. She couldn't like the staff nurse who had never been kind or friendly and there was that little throb of jealousy whenever she thought of her and Ross in passionate embrace. She couldn't even take comfort from the belief that he had broken with Georgy when she compared her very ordinary prettiness and unexciting self with those glowing good looks and that vivid personality. But if Georgy knew only a fraction of her feeling for Ross, then she couldn't help a certain sympathy with the staff nurse.

Pulse and temps, washings and bedpans, taking one patient to Theatres and another to Radiography and a host of other chores that made her wish that she had another pair of hands at least, caused the morning to pass very quickly for Phyllida. Kevin was in and out of the ward several times, apparently too busy to talk and scarcely managing a smile which surprised her, but there was no sign of Ross by the time that she went to lunch. But they had admitted two of the Professor's patients that morning so he would probably visit the ward sometime during the day. She hoped it wouldn't be while she was away from it.

She made her way by roundabout route to the juniors' dining room, lingering in corridors and looking hopefully through open doors, knowing that he must be somewhere in the hospital. No doubt he was busy on other wards or delayed in Outpatients with a longer than usual clinic. Perhaps he was as impatient as herself with circumstances that kept them from seeing each other.

Returning to Paterson, her heart recognised him by the merest whisk of a white coat turning a corner. She quickened her steps to catch him before he could enter the ward. Reaching the swing doors, he glanced over his shoulder at the sound of her step and held the door for her with an automatic courtesy. But he neither smiled nor spoke and her own smile was checked by the coldness of the dark eyes and a certain grimness about his mouth. Her heart throbbed with sudden alarm.

'Ross, how are you?' she asked warmly, voice low so that no one should hear the familiar greeting of a first year for a senior doctor.

He nodded, curt. 'How's the ankle?'

He sounded so indifferent that she was stunned, shaken. 'Fine . . . it's fine,' she returned, almost stumbling on the words.

Her anxious eyes searched the good-looking but suddenly discouraging face for reassurance but found none. She told herself hastily that he was being formal because they were both on duty. But it was hard to believe it when he looked at her as though they had never been friends let alone lovers.

'Glad to hear it.' He walked away from her briskly, making his way to the desk where Georgy was sitting, in charge of the ward while Sister was at lunch.

He didn't sound glad, Phyllida thought in dismay, observing the way he smiled at Georgy and the almost-surprised but certainly delighted way that the staff nurse smiled back. He bent low to speak to her, so obviously a private and meaningful murmur that Phyllida's heart contracted painfully.

It seemed that he had gone back to Georgy's arms as if he had never left them, his brief fancy for herself ending as abruptly as it had begun. She had been a fool to believe one word of his lies or the magic of his sensuous embrace. He had not missed her at all in the last few days. He had probably not given her another thought after leaving her that day at her home. Out of sight really did mean out of mind—and out of heart where he was concerned, she thought unhappily.

She hurried into the sluice and ran taps and clattered bedpans to seem busy, struggling with the wave of misery and despair that came from loving and trusting a man like Ross.

Surely he couldn't brush her aside like a nothing in his life—not now! Not when she had given so much, so gladly!

He was busy, preoccupied. They were both on duty and it was difficult to exchange warm and meaningful words. He hadn't meant to seem so cold and indifferent. As for Georgy, she had probably read too much into his continued friendliness towards someone who had so recently been a lover. Didn't she know just how nice he could be?

Ross just wasn't the cold and heartless and utterly selfish monster that people made him out to be! She knew he could be warm and kind and considerate. She had seen a side to him that other people wouldn't believe to exist. She knew he had come near to loving when he held her, kissed her, made tender and wonderful love to her. A woman knew in her blood and her bones and the very heart of her when she mattered to a man! She wouldn't believe that it was all over before it had hardly begun! He must want her still!

'There you are, Nurse Sims! Why didn't you report to me when you came back to the ward?' Georgy glowered, finding fault where there was none. 'Mrs Butler has had an accident with her tea and her bed needs changing. Don't dawdle now!'

Phyllida abandoned the bedpans and sped to the linen cupboard for clean bedding, burning with dislike and resentment of the staff nurse who glowed with such obvious self-satisfaction and still couldn't find a kind word for a junior.

She helped the apologetic Mrs Butler out of bed and into a chair and stripped off the sheets. Helen Buckley helped her to make up the bed afresh. The curtains were drawn about the next bed as Ross questioned and examined one of the new admissions. Phyllida could just distinguish the murmur of his deep voice. She wondered if he would redeem himself and raise her spirits by making an opportunity to speak to her warmly before he left the ward.

Georgy put her head round the curtains. 'Nurse Sims, lay up a catheterization trolley and bring it here immediately.'

'Yes, Staff.' Phyllida hastily eased the overweight Mrs Butler back against the pillows, tucked in the sheets and hurried to the clinical room. She seized a trolley and reached for instruments and sterile packs of swabs and towels, receivers and lotion and scissors, trying to remember and set out in proper order all the items that Ross needed to catheterize his patient.

Georgy ran a professionally critical eye over the laid trolley as Phyllida wheeled it into the cubicle, carefully not looking at Ross who listened with an understanding expression as the patient complained of the inconvenience of coming into hospital when her eldest was getting married and her youngest had just left school and was bound to get into mischief, hanging about the streets with his friends.

'You'll be home again before you know it, Mrs Ellis—and well enough to dance at your daughter's wedding,' Ross told her reassuringly.

'Where are the catheters, Nurse?' Georgy was ominously patient with an idiot of a junior who had forgotten the most necessary item of all.

Ross turned to look at Phyllida. Meeting his eyes, she saw that there wasn't a grain of humour in them. Having lost all interest, he couldn't even be amused by her awful and consistent incompetence any more, she thought sadly, remembering how that sympathetic twinkle had eased many a bad moment for her in the past.

Heat rising in her face, she stammered: 'I've forgotten them . . . I'm sorry, Staff. I'll go and get them . . .'

Feeling a fool, she turned hastily and barged into the trolley. It tilted and the bottle of antiseptic lotion crashed to the floor. Making a grab to save the trolley, Phyllida slipped and fell against the bed, jolting the startled patient. She scrambled to her feet, hot with embarrassment and cold with dismay, and put a hand to the locker for support, knocking over the water jug.

Longing to cap it all by conveniently falling through the floor, she stared aghast at the trail of disaster in her wake. Georgy glared and snapped a sharp rebuke. Mrs Ellis muttered an unsympathetic tch of exaspera-ation.

Saving the situation for Phyllida, the pager in the registrar's breast pocket began to 'bleep'. With an abrupt apology to the patient, Ross thrust back the curtains and strode down the ward, encountering the returned Sister Hamilton who was hurrying to investi-gate the disturbance.

'Paterson is rapidly turning into the worst run ward of my experience,' he said coldly, too angry to weigh his words. 'I wonder how some of the first-years manage to get through their preliminary training!'

'Oh dear! Nurse Sims!' she said in swift and rueful comprehension. He continued down the ward to her desk. She put her head round the curtains and took in the situation at a glance. 'I'll speak to you in my office, Nurse Sims,' she said, very brisk. 'Leave what you are doing. Nurse Knight will attend to it.' Georgy bridled but she could not protest. Phyllida fled and Sister Hamil-ton turned to reassure the incensed patient. 'The doctor has been called away, Mrs Ellis. He'll be back very soon and nurse will make you comfortable in the mean-time . . .'

Ross was talking into the telephone as Phyllida hur-ried past the desk, obviously near to tears. She didn't look at him. He turned his shoulder slightly so that their eyes shouldn't meet even by chance. He didn't mean to weaken or he would have done so when he heard her voice saying his name so warmly when he answered the telephone in his flat. It had cost him something then to brush her off, to hang up. It had cost him even more to acknowledge her on the ward as though they were little more than strangers.

Just now, he was very annoyed with her. For there was nothing more likely to shatter a patient's confidence than a fumbling, stumbling nurse causing riot and rumpus around her bed. He was beginning to despair that Phyllida would ever overcome her natural tendency for disaster. It was strange when she was not really a clumsy or awkward girl. He had been impressed by her natural grace and she was not lacking in confidence. But let loose on a ward full of unsuspecting patients, she went to pieces!

She would never make a nurse. It seemed very likely that she wouldn't stay at Hartlake long enough to finish her training, anyway. Like too many of the juniors, she would get married and give up nursing.

Ross didn't want to think how much he would miss her if that happened. He told himself firmly that it wasn't going to be too difficult to thrust her out of his life and forget all about her in the arms of other girls. But just now it was hard to shut out the image of that pretty, flushed and dismayed face, urging him to hurry after her and offer a little comfort.

He dragged his attention from the departing first-year and back to the casualty officer with a problem in Accident and Emergency.

'Very well. I'll be right down,' he said, replacing the receiver. On his way from the ward, he passed Sister's office and glanced through the open door to see Phyllida standing by the desk, waiting for her scold. Tempted to pause, to speak to her, he walked on, hardening his heart.

Phyllida was trying to rehearse some kind of explanation and apology for Sister. Seeing him pass the door, she swallowed her pride and hurried to call after him. 'Ross!'

He ignored the plea in her voice and carried on down the corridor. Phyllida looked after him in utter dismay. Nothing could be clearer than that snub, more pointed than any of the rebuffs he had dealt out in the early days of unimportant misunderstandings.

Impulsively, she ran after him and caught at his arm, forgetting Sister and everything else in the need to understand why he had ceased to want her.

'Ross! What is it? What's happened? Why won't you talk to me?'

He looked down at her, impatient, a little annoyed that she forced him to be blunt. 'I'm due in A and E. I haven't time to talk to you!'

What did she expect him to say, anyway? Did she think he was going to gratify her vanity by begging her to love him, to want him, to marry him instead of Lawson? No woman could bring him to his knees in such fashion no matter how important she might seem to be in the first flush of new and rather unwelcome loving.

'Or inclination,' Phyllida said carefully, shattered by his obvious impatience that relegated her to the unimportant past.

'At least I don't have to spell it out for you.' He was coolly dismissive.

Her heart faltered. 'Is it . . . Georgy?' She couldn't think of any other reason why he had suddenly lost interest, suddenly ceased to want her at all.

Ross certainly didn't mean to admit that it was disappointment and dismay. He didn't mean to tell her that her engagement to Lawson had shattered all his illusions about her and convinced him that he had been a fool to feel that she was different, the one girl in the world he could trust with the heart that had always been so reluctant to love. It was easier to let her suppose that he had decided to prefer the beautiful and sophisticated and very sexy Georgy. A sop for his pride.

He smiled, sardonic. 'But it always was Georgy, darling,' he said, very light and mocking. 'I never made any secret of that.'

Her hand shot out of its own volition and slapped him, hard. How could he call her '*darling*' for the very first time in just that sneering and very hurtful way? How could he throw her love back at her so cruelly and make her feel cheap because it had been so obviously just a sex thing for him, short-lived and quite meaningless? How could he live up to all the things that people said about him and which she had so stubbornly refused to believe because she loved him?

The marks of her fingers stood out on his lean cheek. His eyes had darkened but he continued to smile. She didn't see how tightly his hands were clenched in the pockets of his coat.

'I guess you feel you owed me that,' he drawled, tense with anger but understanding that swift and instinctive reaction of a girl who had surrendered her virginity only to regret it. He had not really taken anything from her, he felt. She had chosen to give it. But, like so many women, she needed to thrust the blame for her own sensuality on to his shoulders.

'Nurse Sims!'

Before Phyllida could tell him what she thought of him, Sister Hamilton's voice, shaking with anger, told them both that she had witnessed a scene that should never have taken place in a hospital corridor. A nurse did not strike another member of the profession, whatever the provocation—and certainly not within the hallowed walls of Hartlake!

Ross stalked off without another word and Phyllida turned to face the wrath of a woman she liked and respected.

Short-staffed though they were, busy though they might be, Sister Hamilton had no intention of keeping such an irresponsible, ill-behaved nurse on her ward and said so without mincing matters.

Phyllida didn't even try to defend herself. She was much too miserable.

'I am sending you off duty, Nurse. You will report to Matron tomorrow morning to explain your behaviour to her. And I'm very much inclined to tell Matron that I no longer want you on my ward at all,' Sister finished, thoroughly cross and very disappointed.

She would never make a nurse, Phyllida thought unhappily, taking off the crisp white apron that was the recognised symbol of a nurse on duty, and preparing to make her way meekly back to the Nurses' Home to fill in the anxious hours before she reported to Matron. To be suspended from duty was going to be a very black mark on her record, she knew. It was such a pity when she was trying so hard to be a good nurse.

Perhaps she should resign, pack her bags and go home to forget all about nursing and Ross. It might not be too difficult to forget her cherished ambition to be a Hartlake nurse. She knew she wouldn't forget Ross as long as she lived.

She didn't understand him. She didn't know why he behaved as he did. She didn't want to believe that he was as heartless as he seemed. She knew she would always love him, anyway . . .

CHAPTER THIRTEEN

PHYLLIDA couldn't settle to anything that evening. She didn't feel there was any point in studying when she didn't know if she would be needing her books in the future. For Matron might insist on her resignation. Hartlake might feel that it just couldn't cope with someone who wreaked so much havoc in so short a time on one of its busy wards, she thought ruefully.

She was apprehensive about facing Matron. But she felt quite sick with dismay when she learned from her friends that it was common knowledge that she had bandied insults with Ross Harman on the ward and then slapped his face in front of the patients and Sister Hamilton.

As usual, the grapevine had distorted the facts. But if that particular version had reached Matron's ears then it would probably mean instant dismissal.

More important, Ross must be furious. Such an incident couldn't help his career or further his standing with some of his junior colleagues. Phyllida wished that she hadn't slapped him so impulsively. It hadn't eased her heartache and humiliation in the least and now there was no way that they could even be friends. He would probably never speak to her again.

Left to herself, she would have sunk into the depths of depression. But her friends wouldn't allow it. Telling her that the whole thing would be forgotten in a few days if she made light of it, they persuaded her to cock a snook at the gossips and go with them as planned to the disco at the social club.

The Administration Wing at Hartlake was a modern building that contained not only offices but also a ball-room that was used for a variety of functions, a swim-ming pool and indoor squash and tennis courts and various clubs that nurses and medical students were encouraged to join although anti-social shifts of duty meant that they couldn't always take advantage of the many events. The weekly disco that was organised by the staff social club was one of the most popular of its events among the younger members of staff. It was held in a room adjoining a bar with comfortable chairs and a pleasant atmosphere. It was a popular meeting place and very crowded that evening.

Phyllida was sure that heads turned and that everyone was talking about the girl who would probably go down in Hartlake history as the first-year nurse who had slapped a senior registrar's face before a ward full of patients. She was glad to reach the comparative obscur-ity of the disco with its pulsating coloured lights and compelling beat of the music. She had never felt less like dancing and her heart was much too heavy to enjoy anything but at least she could merge with the crowd.

Among the crowd, she saw Kevin, so distinctive with his blond head that seemed to reflect the vivid colours of the flashing lights. He was with friends, laughing and talking, his arm about the waist of a girl she didn't know. She felt a slight wrench of dismay. Had he deserted her, too?

She remembered that he had only smiled and not

spoken to her on the ward although they hadn't seen each other for some days. So much for the absurd rumour that they were engaged! She ought to be relieved and glad if he had found someone else, of course—for his sake. But it was rather shattering to be suddenly bereft of both the men in her life, she thought wryly.

Catching Kevin's eye, she smiled at him in friendly, undemanding fashion. He didn't owe her any loyalty, after all, she reminded herself, knowing a twinge of guilt that she had kept him so firmly at a distance when he loved her and allowed Ross who didn't love her at all to take her to bed.

With a word to his friends, Kevin left them and made his way through the crush of dancers to reach her side. 'Hallo, love,' he said lightly, just as naturally as if her affair with Ross Harman was not in the forefront of his mind these days. He was hurt and disappointed but he sensed that she needed him right now and he cared enough to support her. He smiled at her with affection and a hint of sympathetic understanding.

Phyllida almost fell on his neck in gratitude that he was still her friend. She was fond of him and she valued his affection. She clung tightly to the hand that reached out and captured her own. 'I'm glad that you're talking to me,' she said with a rueful laugh. 'I thought I was in disgrace with everyone.' There was no need to wonder if he had heard the gossip. It was all over Hartlake.

'I'm on your side,' Kevin told her firmly. 'I've been ready to punch Harman's nose for days. It's about time somebody put him in his place. I know you liked him and didn't believe what people said about him. But I thought you'd find out for yourself that he's a bastard.' He squeezed her hand. 'If he's hurt you I *will* punch his nose for him!' he added savagely, meaning it.

Phyllida was moved by his concern. Ross had hurt her far more than she would ever want anyone to know. For the sake of her pride, she must convince Kevin and everyone else that it had been a very minor involvement on her part. For the rest of the evening, she did her best . . .

Ross was duty registrar. For once, A and E wasn't particularly busy and he made his way to the Administration Wing and the club to relax for half an hour with a beer and a sandwich, expecting to be 'bleeped' at any moment. He had forgotten the disco and was surprised to find the bar lounge so crowded. He found a quiet corner as far as possible from the disco, trying to ignore the loud blast of music every time the doors opened to admit or let out the dancers.

He nodded or spoke briefly to colleagues and friends who paused by his chair but he was so obviously in no mood to be sociable that they soon drifted away. He knew that people were talking about his contretemps with Phyllida that afternoon. The grapevine had been busy with his affairs so often that he could dismiss the latest buzz of speculation with a shrug of his broad shoulders. He found it impossible to dismiss the blow to his heart and his pride that she had dealt him.

He couldn't understand why a girl who seemed so honest and so straightforward should have deceived him quite deliberately about her relationship with the house-man. And it puzzled him that a girl presumably in love with a man she had promised to marry should give herself so readily to him when she was obviously not a

wanton. He knew without a shadow of doubt that she
had been a virgin until that evening at his flat.

Ross had never known such tumult of wanting for any
other woman. The mere thought of her in Lawson's arms
filled him with a raging despair. He was consumed with
love for a girl who didn't love him at all and he thought
bitterly that he was paid back in his own coin for all the
times that he had taken what he wanted with loveless
sensuality without a thought for the impact of his brief
attentions on a girl's heart. Phyllida had given her lovely
body with a warm and generous yielding that had en-
chanted and delighted him and swept him into aware-
ness of what it meant to love. But she had kept her heart
for another man—and it was her heart that he wanted
more than anything else in the world.

Suddenly he saw her, emerging from the disco with
Lawson, laughing up at the houseman as though she
didn't have a care in the world—and why should she
have? She was in love and engaged to be married and the
future must seem very bright for Phyllida. It seemed
very bleak to him.

Ross leaped from his chair and strode towards the
door, wishing that he hadn't come into the club that
evening. Then he wouldn't have seen her, looking so
radiantly happy and so lovely that the loss of her was
suddenly too much to bear . . .

Out of the corner of her eye, Phyllida saw the tall
figure in the long white coat heading for the exit and
knew before she turned that it had to be Ross because of
the way her heart lurched—and knew, too, that she had
to speak to him even at the risk of another hurtful rebuff.

Abandoning the startled Kevin without a word of

explanation, Phyllida impulsively flew after the departing registrar. He took the door that led out to the hospital garden. She lost him for a moment in the shadows and stood, hesitant. Then she saw him on the paved path that cut across the lawns to the main building.

Heart pounding, she ran across the grass to catch at his arm just as he reached the statue of Sir Henry. Ross swung round, surprised and suspicious, so lost in despairing thought that he hadn't realised her approach. 'What the devil . . . ?' he demanded angrily before he saw that it was Phyllida.

She thought she saw the flicker of anger in his eyes. Courage almost failed but the desperation of her feelings drove her to swallow her pride just as she had done before for this man's sake. Loving him left no room for pride in her heart.

'Not the devil . . . me!' she said, forcing a smile.

He raised an eyebrow. 'Well?'

It wasn't encouraging. Phyllida refused to be discouraged by the cool tone, by the resistance she sensed in him. 'Don't brush me off,' she said, carefully light. 'I won't keep you more than a minute or two. That's all it takes to say sorry.'

He stiffened. 'What makes you think I regret anything?'

'Not you!' she exclaimed hastily. 'Me!' She was so tense she was gripping his arm very tightly. Neither of them noticed. 'I'm sorry—really I am!'

So she knew how much she had hurt him, disappointed him. She knew that she had struck a devastating blow at his pride. Perhaps she hadn't meant things to go so far between them. Perhaps she had only been playing with fire—and then found herself consumed by its flame!

'So am I,' he said quietly.

She thought he regretted that they had been lovers. Perhaps he had discovered that he was in love with Georgy and wished he hadn't betrayed her in another girl's arms. Perhaps he would never have made love to her if she hadn't thrown herself at him so blatantly that it had been impossible for him or any red-blooded male to refuse what she was offering. Perhaps he despised her—and himself.

'Don't . . . don't hate me,' she said, her voice unsteady.

That little tremor caught at his heart. No matter what she was, what she had done, he couldn't help loving her. He put an arm about her and drew her against him in a warm embrace. 'Silly girl,' he said, roughly, and kissed her gently. 'Does that seem like hate?' he asked wryly.

Maybe it wasn't hate but it certainly wasn't love, either, Phyllida thought despairingly. Knowing how she felt about him, he was sorry for her. She had tasted the sorrow of compassion on his lips—and she didn't want it! She wanted him to love her as she loved him, to want her as she wanted him, to feel as she did that nothing was worth anything unless they were together until the end of time!

She tried not to cling to him but it was hard to pull out of the arms that she wanted so much to have about her for the rest of her life. He was so nice, so generous, so ready to forgive her for the slap whose echo had reverberated all over Hartlake and caused such a furore. It was not his fault that he cared more for Georgy than for her—and she reminded herself that he had never claimed to care for her at all. He had never made any secret of what he wanted from her, after all. It had been a foolish first-year's fancy that he was near to loving her when she had only been one more sexual conquest for a very sensual and much too attractive man.

She smiled at him bravely. 'I know we can't go back to being friends,' she said brightly. 'But I want you to know that I don't regret that we were lovers. It was a marvellous experience.'

As always, he was moved by her unexpected honesty and by the warm generosity of her impulsive giving. He reached to cradle her head in his strong hand in a tender caress, a smile in his eyes. 'For me, too,' he said, very low. He bent to touch her lips very lightly with his own. 'You really were something special, Phyllida . . .'

She recognised words and kiss as the finality of farewell. Pain, radiating from the very core of her being, engulfed her in a moment. She didn't dare to stay another second or she would embarrass them both by throwing her arms about him and begging him through her tears to stay with her and love her and need her. She backed away from him and then turned and ran for the sanctuary of the shadows.

Ross looked after her, torn between the need to call her back into his arms and the realisation that she had been near to tears with compassion for him. She was so sweet, so soft-hearted, so generous with her affection. It was not her fault that she loved Lawson and therefore could not love him, he thought heavily. He had been just a fleeting fancy for a first-year, so new to the game of love that she had been swept off her feet by the tidal wave of unexpected and hard-to-handle desire. Loving her, he had to let her go because he had no right to call her back. Only husbands and fiancés had rights. Merely casual lovers had no rights at all . . .

Phyllida's apron was spotless, her uniform frock as crisp as could be, her cap set precisely atop severely brushed curls and her black brogues gleamed with polish as she prepared to humble herself before Matron.

She gave a last glance at herself in the mirror of the juniors' room on Paterson and then hurried along the corridor to report to Sister Hamilton in obedience to the message conveyed to her by Sister Vernon that morning.

She knocked and was bidden to enter.

Sister Hamilton looked her over briefly and continued to write out discharge certificates for those patients who were well enough to go home that day.

Phyllida waited, hands demurely behind her back in approved fashion and wearing a suitably chastened expression.

Sister Hamilton laid down her pen and studied her for a long moment. Then she said quietly: 'I expect you will be relieved to know that I decided not to report you to Matron, after all.'

Phyllida's eyes brightened and she visibly relaxed. 'Oh, yes, Sister! Thank you, Sister!' she said in heartfelt tones.

The older woman covered an involuntary smile with a slight, contrived cough. 'That doesn't mean that I'm not very displeased with you, Nurse Sims,' she said sternly.

'Yes, Sister. I'm very sorry, Sister.'

She was so obviously contrite that this time the ward sister allowed a glimmer of her smile to show through. 'So I should hope,' she said briskly. 'I am appalled that any nurse on my ward should behave so badly.' Phyllida bit her lip and said nothing. 'Well, you may thank Mr Harman for persuading me against my better judgment to say nothing to Matron! I don't wish to know anything about your quarrel with him and you may believe that he didn't enlighten me except to say very definitely that he offered the utmost provocation and it wasn't fair that you should be penalised. Your personal life is your business, Nurse. But it doesn't belong on my ward. Do you understand?'

'Yes, Sister. It won't happen again,' she promised fervently, astonished and touched that Ross should have intervened on her behalf and wondering why he hadn't told her so last night.

'As for the other business, you will apologise to Nurse Knight for upsetting the entire ward in my absence.'

Phyllida's face flamed. 'Sister, I do try but nothing goes right when Nurse Knight is in charge,' she blurted with her usual impulsive candour. 'She doesn't like me and she makes me nervous and I feel that she's just waiting for me to do silly things and so I do them!'

Sister picked up her pen and took a fresh certificate from the box on her desk. She had no intention of allowing a first-year nurse to criticise her right hand on the ward even if she cherished a secret sympathy for the juniors who suffered from Georgy Knight's sharp tongue and overbearing manner.

'You have a lot to learn about nursing and you can't expect to be popular with efficient and very professional senior nurses in the meantime,' she said briskly. 'Now run along and help with rounds, Nurse Sims. We have six patients going to Theatres today and we shall be very busy. Please do your best to be a useful member of my ward staff. Try to make haste without rushing about the ward like a bull in a china shop,' she added dryly with just the hint of a twinkle in her eyes.

'Yes, Sister. Thank you, Sister . . .'

Phyllida had been dreading the interview with Matron who was a very formidable lady. Her heart was considerably lighter as she left Sister's office and went into the ward. She had almost convinced herself that she would have to leave Hartlake and the thought had depressed her. For she did enjoy nursing and she did feel that she could turn into a good nurse with time. But, most of all, she needed to be within sight and sound of Ross even if loving him was never going to bring her any happiness at all.

She had spent much of the night in recalling that brief encounter in the shadows of the hospital garden. There had been some comfort for her aching heart in remembering the way he had held her head with that warmly tender hand, the tenderness in his kiss and in his voice as he told her that she had been something special in his life. If only it was true. He had made it seem true. Not only last night but when she had lain in his arms and known the glorious ecstasy of his love-making.

Perhaps it had always been foolish and futile self-deception, just an absurd fancy, but it had seemed that they had a wealth of loving to give each other, she thought sadly. With his arms about her, Georgy and all the others had faded into the limbo of the forgotten and unimportant past and she had felt that she might be his future.

What a fool she had been to suppose that she could compete with the beautiful and self-assured and very sophisticated Georgy! The staff nurse was so obviously the kind of girl that a man like Ross would choose to love out of all the many women he had known. Casual conquests like herself had to accept that they played no real part in a Casanova's life . . .

Mrs Ellis was going to Theatres that morning and Ross made a brief visit to the ward to check for himself that the self-retaining catheter he had inserted for post-operative drainage of the urinary tract was still properly in position and to write up a drug to safeguard against infection after surgery.

Phyllida was helping Georgy Knight with the drugs round, carefully checking each dosage and taking the tablets or medicine to the patients.

When she returned the drugs trolley to its usual position opposite the ward desk, securely locked after the round, Ross was talking to Sister about the need for careful observation of Mrs Ellis when she returned from Theatres.

Sister broke off briefly to pick up a sheet of paper from the desk. 'Nurse! Take this to Theatre Sister, please— and don't dawdle. She's waiting for this list.'

'Yes, Sister . . .' With the memory of her encounter with Ross on the ward of the previous day too vivid in her mind and, she suspected, in Sister Hamilton's as well, Phyllida didn't dare to look at the registrar.

He was on his way to Theatres but he didn't offer to

take the list. He thanked Sister for her time with his usual smiling courtesy and strode after the first-year with an air of purpose. Sister Hamilton looked after them both with amused resignation and thought that she must be getting sentimental in her old age to throw opportunities in their way . . .

Conscious that he was close on her heels, Phyllida held the swing doors for him. He thanked her with his swift and very attractive smile and her heart missed a beat. 'I wanted to thank you,' she said impulsively. 'Sister told me that you persuaded her not to report me and I'm very grateful, Ross. Matron would have wiped the floor with me.'

'I expect Lawson gave you an uncomfortable half-hour,' he said dryly. 'No man likes to think that his fiancée has been tangling with someone like me.'

Phyllida looked up at him quickly. 'I'm not engaged to Kevin!'

His eyes narrowed abruptly. 'That isn't what I heard!'

'I know it's what people were saying but it isn't true,' she said urgently. She was horrified that he had believed that ridiculous snippet of gossip. At the same time, her heart lifted with a sudden, tremulous hope that a misunderstanding about her relationship with Kevin might be more to blame for his sudden, surprising indifference than a preference for Georgy Knight.

'But you are in love with him?' He was brusque, almost accusing. 'That's true, isn't it?'

Phyllida shook her head. 'No. How could it be? I love you,' she said simply. 'I thought you knew.'

Ross was taken completely by surprise but he realised that he should have known it because a girl like Phyllida, all heart and integrity, would never give herself so readily to a man she didn't love.

A passing nurse glanced at them curiously. A hospital corridor was not the place for lovers, he thought wryly . . . but Sister's sitting-room was right at hand and she was busy on the ward. He took Phyllida by the arm and whisked her into the room and closed the door firmly.

'I didn't know,' he said wryly, standing with his back to the door. He regarded her with a rueful smile in the depths of his dark eyes. 'Not knowing has been hell!'

He reached out to catch her close, to hold her so tightly that her breasts were crushed painfully against his hard chest. She didn't even notice, only aware with a swelling heart of the love and the unmistakable tenderness in the way he held her.

He had never expected to know this tumult of love for any woman. But Phyllida wasn't like other women. She was special with her warm and loving heart, her sweet and generous nature, her incorruptible integrity. He would love her for the rest of his life—and he told her so, quietly and with conviction.

Phyllida clung to him in incredulous and delighted thanksgiving for the fulfilment of an impossible dream. She turned her face to kiss the cheek that she had slapped because she loved him and couldn't bear the thought of losing him.

'Do you really love me?' she asked on a little sigh, seeking reassurance like any woman in love.

'Oh, Phyllida . . .' The tenderness in his tone turned her name into a memorable and very precious endearment. 'What do I have to do to make you believe me?'

She drew away from him slightly and looked up at him

with a little dancing delight in her deep blue eyes.

'You could k-kiss me,' she suggested with deceptive demurity and a deliberate little stammer to remind him of that evening in his flat when lovers for a brief hour had become lovers for all time.

His lips came down on her own with all the promise of real and lasting happiness that any woman could want . . . and the list for Theatre Sister fell to the floor and was forgotten . . .

How to join in a whole new world of romance

It's very easy to subscribe to the Mills & Boon Reader Service. As a regular reader, you can enjoy a whole range of special benefits. Bargain offers. Big cash savings. Your own free Reader Service newsletter, packed with knitting patterns, recipes, competitions, and exclusive book offers.

We send you the very latest titles each month, postage and packing free – no hidden extra charges. There's absolutely no commitment – you receive books for only as long as you want.

We'll send you details. Simply send the coupon – or drop us a line for details about the Mills & Boon Reader Service Subscription Scheme. Post to: Mills & Boon Reader Service, P.O. Box 236, Thornton Road, Croydon, Surrey CR9 3RU, England. *Please note: READERS IN SOUTH AFRICA please write to: Mills & Boon Reader Service of Southern Africa, Private Bag X3010, Randburg 2125, S. Africa.

Please send me details of the Mills & Boon Subscription Scheme.

NAME (Mrs/Miss) _____ EP3

ADDRESS _____

_____

COUNTY/COUNTRY_____ POST/ZIP CODE_____

BLOCK LETTERS, PLEASE

Mills & Boon
the rose of romance